Green Gravy, Monster Bread and Other Adventures

Green Gravy, Monster Bread and Other Adventures

Alice Breon

Library of Congress Control Number: 2011918134
ISBN: Hardcover   978-1-4653-7725-8
                 Softcover   978-1-4653-7724-1
                 Ebook   978-1-4653-7726-5

This book was printed in the United States of America.

To order additional copies of this book, contact:
Xlibris Corporation
1-888-795-4274
www.Xlibris.com
Orders@Xlibris.com
86163

Contents

For my children and their children.

PREFACE

Y OU HAVE HAD experiences and circumstances in your life that combine to make you who you are. You have a story to pass on to your children, grandchildren, nieces, and nephews. Future generations will have no idea about what the world was like when you were growing up if you don't share it. And since we all have had different experiences, there is a wealth of information just waiting to be told.

Each generation sees social and economic changes and new developments in technology. As new concepts appear, some of the popular and well-loved customs of the earlier generations fade away. The toys that today's children play with are entirely different from the toys in the 1950s. The teenagers who will graduate from high school in 2012 have no idea what a phonograph record is.

My parents' generation saw the invention of the telephone, phonograph, automobile, airplane, radio, and movies. In 1920, the women won the right to vote. Following this freedom, women discarded the traditional long full skirts and petticoats and started a new style with skirts above the knee. They had their long hair cut short in what was called the "bob." That era was called the roaring twenties.

We can read about these developments in history books, but when I found my father's diary, I gained an insight that history books could never capture. My father came to the

United States from Sweden when he was twenty-four years old. He wrote in a diary during the nine-day trip on the ship. He traveled in third class and described everything he saw and what his impressions were. I read about the Danes, Norwegians, and Swedes who danced every night on deck. The single women left the dancing before dark. Their sleeping quarters were at the front of the ship, and men were not allowed near there.

He described the dolphins that swam beside the ship and the Irish people who played accordions and sang their native songs one stormy night. All the things he wrote about gave me a new perspective of what it was like to live during that time.

My generation lived through the Great Depression, World War II, and three other conflicts. We saw the invention of television, computers, and cell phones.

There were rapid advances in medicine, starting with the development of penicillin and the polio vaccine. We witnessed the civil rights movement, the Kennedy assassination, and the landing on the moon. Who can imagine what future generations are going to discover and invent?

I have told stories of my childhood and adult years to my grandchildren, and I think they learned a bit of history from these stories, but they also discovered that life was different when Grandma was growing up.

So write your story and give the future generation a glimpse of your world when you were a child and a young adult. You are unique. You have stories that only you can tell.

FOREWORD

MY AUNT ALICE told many of the stories collected here over the years at family gatherings. It's a treasure to have them brought together in one place because they not only are wise and witty but also offer important insights into the situation of women, children, and families of "the Greatest Generation," as those citizens who came of age during World War 2 and who then led the way into the cold war years have been called.

I knew my aunt Alice as "Alice Marie" or "Little Alice" in childhood. She was my babysitter on occasion, which I don't remember clearly, and sometimes played with me (which I do remember as lots of fun) until she married and moved across the country. After that: the special holiday phone call, some visits, and shared family vacations with my cousins before they went to Japan. At that point things became very postmodern: Alice sent back a small Japanese tape recorder (which we'd never seen before) so Grandpa and all the rest of us could actually hear everyone overseas. The little tapes kept coming and kept us up to date. Alice had already been making little 8mm home movies, so this was a continuation of her media artistry. When the family returned to the States, we got to also hear the stories and see home movies of life in Japan. I remember the cherry blossoms and my cousin Barbara, a little blond, in her school uniform standing out in a class of her black-haired Japanese peers.

Most of the Greatest Generation historical narrative has been told about men, especially those who served in combat, in the form of journalism, in history books, in novels, and in films. Here we have the other side, the story of a young woman who saw most of the young men in her high school class immediately leave for military service. The dominant story of the postwar aftermath has also been told as the story of men with sometimes a glamorous role for a celebrity female. Alice's stories cover a different terrain, one which takes her halfway around the world to Japan. But the stories are at the core of domestic life, especially for the wife of an air force officer who was frequently immersed in secret and urgent work. Like most military wives and mothers, Alice had to use imagination, pluckiness, and fortitude to make a rich family life. And she did.

These stories not only reveal her unique personality and creativity but also supply a missing story and a sharp contrast to stereotyped and fictional versions of Americans abroad in the 1950s and '60s. Here the texture of daily life appears, and cross-cultural exchange and new experience takes on a personal tone. These stories, often comic, sometimes poignant, even heartbreaking, show how people-to-people relations, whatever the cultural and political differences present, can showcase the best of our humanity and love.

Chuck Kleinhans
September 2011
Eugene, Oregon

ACKNOWLEDGMENTS

I WOULD LIKE to express my sincere gratitude to the following people for their help:

Fujiko Signs who reviewed the chapters about Japan for accuracy and inspired me to write more about her native country.

Debbie Fredley, Libby Walizer, and Carter Ackerman, who were always available to help me navigate the complex world of the computer.

My children, Buz, Ken, and Barbara, who often said, "Don't forget to write about ..."

Charles Kleinhans and Julia LeSage whose judgment I value.

Finally, Lurene Frantz and the ladies of the Christmas luncheon group who listened to my stories and said, "You should write a book." So I did.

1

The Day Our Lives Changed

But this was Yoshiko's country with its own set of standards and traditions.

I couldn't advise her, and I couldn't surmise what her answer would be.

At long last, I heard the front door close. I waited a few minutes, then cautiously walked down the hall to the living room. Yoshiko was standing with her back to me, facing the door.

"Yoshiko?"
"Yes."
"Did you decide?"
"Yes."
"Are you getting married?"

She turned around, her eyes filled with tears. I opened my arms and held her while her heart broke.

"DECEMBER 7TH, 1941, a date which will live in infamy—"

Our high school was holding a mandatory assembly in the gymnasium. All of us were seated on folding chairs when the special broadcast from President Roosevelt came over the loudspeakers.

It was Monday, December 8, 1941. I was sixteen years old, a junior that year. All of us already knew about the attack on Pearl Harbor the day before. We talked about it on the school bus and as we walked to our homerooms. At our homerooms, we were told to go to the gymnasium for a special radio broadcast from the president of the United States.

"The United States of America was suddenly and deliberately attacked by naval and air forces of the Empire of Japan. I ask that the Congress declare that since the unprovoked and dastardly attack by Japan on Sunday, December 7th, 1941, a state of war has existed between the United States and the Japanese Empire."

Wikipedia, Franklin D. Roosevelt, Infamy Speech.

We all looked at each other openmouthed. What did this mean? Was there going to be a war right here in the United States? Will we still go to school? We looked at our teachers, hoping they would assure us and give us answers, but they looked just as bewildered as we were.

As we filed into the hallways to go to our classes, we were thoughtful and quiet, not knowing what to expect. A few of the boys in our class said they were going to quit school and sign up for the service, but they were too young. When we reached our classrooms, the teachers started our lessons and carried on as if it were a normal day. I suppose they were as unprepared as we were to face what the future would bring.

Little did I know, at age sixteen, that my future husband was at Hickham Field, Hawaii, while the bombs exploded around him on that fateful day—December 7, 1941.

2

The War Years

A ND SO WE entered the War Years—four long years of sacrifice, praying, worrying, writing letters, and sending care packages to loved ones. By our senior year, many of the boys had reached the age to enlist, and many of them left school and entered the army, navy, or marines. Some of them never came back.

Everyone had a father, brother, cousin, or sweetheart who was away in the service. We watched newsreels at the movies that showed frightening pictures of bombs exploding, invasions on faraway islands, and fighter planes in battle. Gasoline was rationed. Meat, sugar, coffee, and other commodities were needed for the servicemen, so food ration coupons were issued to all families.

The Depression had ended. Factories were converted to making war materials, and there was plenty of work available. However, most able-bodied men were away in the service, so women supplied the workforce. This was a turning point for women. Up until this time, married women stayed at home and kept the household running smoothly.

My brother, Gordon, joined the navy as did all his friends. All my male cousins were in the service. My friends and I made no plans beyond high school. The boys abandoned any preparations for college, and the girls were thinking about joining the Women's Air Force or the Women's

Army Corps. Some of them decided to pursue a nursing career after graduation.

High school continued as usual with football games, homecoming dances, proms. I was a cheerleader and worked on the school newspaper, sang in the a cappella choir, and played violin in the orchestra. I had many friends at school, several very special friends, and various boyfriends.

Our town had two main streets in the downtown area. They were intersected by the Chicago and Northwestern Railroad tracks that led to Chicago. Within the downtown area were a movie theater, library, a small town hall, several churches, two drugstores, a grocery store, butcher shop, and bakery shop. There was also a dress shop, a haberdashery, a millinery, a music store, and Robinson's candy store.

Besides the soda fountain at Robinson's candy store, a favorite teen hangout was the music store. There, with no money spent, one could choose the latest Big Band records, take them to a soundproof booth, and listen to Glenn Miller, Harry James, and Tommy Dorsey for hours. There was even enough room to do a little dancing if the spirit moved you. The proprietor didn't mind if we didn't buy a record after spending all that time in one of the booths. He knew we would eventually buy one when we had the money.

In my junior year, I joined a church-related group of teenagers that was very active socially. The group included boys and girls from several other towns, so we made new friends. We started our first social as a hayride, and from that time on, our group grew in numbers. Everyone heard about our get-togethers and wanted to join. We had scavenger hunts, beach parties at Lake Michigan, Halloween costume dances, bowling parties, sleigh rides, ice skating, and roller-skating parties. We took turns meeting at one another's houses to plan these activities. Our meetings started and ended with prayer for peace and safety of our men in the service.

Fashions had changed during that era. Skirts were shorter, slightly above the knee. Sweaters were long and baggy. Bobby socks and saddle shoes were the common foot-wear. The girls wore their hair long and loose.

The boys had theirs cut short. Some boys sported an extremely short style known as a crew cut.

Girls did not wear slacks to school. Blue jeans were worn by boys, but not for school wear. They were reserved for working outdoors and doing rough manual labor. Girls started wearing blue jeans for the first time around 1942. These were usually snatched from their brothers' rooms as there were no jeans made to fit a woman's figure. Jeans were not a fashion trend, but were worn when hiking or working around the house. They weren't worn when shopping in town or out on a date and certainly not in school.

Alice in her brother's blue jeans

Short plaid skirts, bulky sweaters, saddle shoes.
Standard "uniform" 1941-1946

3

The Movie Star and the Bobby Soxer

R OBERT TAYLOR, CONSIDERED the most handsome actor
ever to grace the silver screen, had left Hollywood during the
war to join the US Naval Air Corps. He was stationed at Glenview Naval
Air Station as a lieutenant, instructing student pilots.

Robert Taylor was my very favorite actor. I was madly in love with him.
The year was 1943, I was a senior in high school, and Glenview Naval Air
Station was about fifteen miles from my house. I found out that my idol
was not living in barracks on the base, but lived at the deluxe Edgewater
Beach Hotel on the shores of Lake Michigan.

I knew I had to meet this gorgeous man, and after much thought, I
devised a plan. I told a girl friend about my plan, and she wanted to join
me. We were going to the Edgewater Beach Hotel disguised as reporters
from the *Chicago Tribune* newspaper. We were going there to interview
Mr. Taylor.

The day we were going to accomplish this deed, we dressed up in
our most adult-looking clothes. I sneaked one of my sister's hats
that I thought made me look very old. After school, armed with our
shorthand notebooks, we rode on a bus for about thirty minutes to get
to the hotel.

I went to the front desk and said, "We're from the *Chicago Tribune,* and
we have an appointment to interview Robert Taylor. What room is he in,

please?" The man at the desk said, "We don't give out that information," and dismissed us.

Not to be discouraged, I saw a bellboy who was about my age, so I went up to him and said, "Do you know which room Robert Taylor is in?" He said, "Yeah, but I can't tell you. I'd lose my job." I pleaded with him until he gave in and told me the room number.

My friend and I took the elevator up to the fourth floor and walked down the hall, looking for the number. I knocked on the door, and we both tried to look like serious reporters.

A woman answered the door and said, "Yeah?" I said, "We're from the *Chicago Tribune* and we'd like to interview Robert Taylor."

She opened the door wide, looked backward, and hollered, "Honey! There's a couple of kids here that want your autograph." A door opened in the apartment, which turned out to be a bathroom door, and there stood Robert Taylor with shaving cream on his face and wearing nothing but his dog tags and his UNDERPANTS!

The woman grabbed our shorthand notebooks and walked over to him. He smiled and waved at us and then signed our books while we stood in the hall, openmouthed, speechless. He handed the books back to the woman, waved and smiled again, and started shaving. The woman said, "I suppose you want my autograph too!" We had no idea who she was, but we nodded, and she signed our books, handed them to us, and shut the door. We ran down the hall until we got to the elevators. Then we looked at the signatures. There was Robert Taylor's autograph and underneath was a signature that was Barbara Stanwyck's. We were very surprised. She was a very popular movie star who always looked beautiful in the movies, but she looked very ordinary in person, especially with no makeup on. She was married to Robert Taylor at that time, but we didn't know about that. I had rather hoped he would wait until he met me before he got married.

Robert Taylor and Barbara Stanwyck have long since gone, but I see their old movies on television, and I distinctly remember gaping at that handsome man who waved to me while wearing his underpants.

Alice, Bobby Soxer

Robert Taylor
Meredy.com/Robert Taylor

4

That Crazy George

I HAD A boyfriend whose name was George, but to my mother, father, aunts, and uncles, his full name was That Crazy George.

My mother lived in constant fear that I would end up marrying That Crazy George, but she needn't have worried. We were teenagers and our main concern was having fun. The serious thought of marriage never entered our heads. George was delightful to be with. We both had the same sense of humor, and we filled the hours with laughter when we were together. He was gregarious, and people loved to have him around (except my mother). He was a good dancer, played all the popular songs on the piano, and was always ready for an adventure.

One Saturday afternoon, we took the train into the "loop" in Chicago. The loop is the very center of Chicago where all the large department stores, elaborate movie theaters, Chicago Civic Opera House, and skyscraper office buildings are. Our town was about fifteen miles northwest of downtown Chicago.

We went to one of the ornate movie theaters where the first-run movies were shown and saw a musical with Danny Kaye and Dinah Shore. There was a great deal of singing and dancing, and we both enjoyed the movie so much we decided to stay for the next show. In those days, you didn't have to leave the theater when the movie was finished. You could stay as long as you wanted.

We watched the second showing, and George ran out to the lobby occasionally to get us some popcorn or candy when we got hungry. After the second show, we talked it over and decided to see the movie one more time because we loved the music and dancing.

By the time we left the theater, it was after 10:00 p.m. and the last train for Park Ridge would be leaving soon. George asked me, "Do you have any money?" Of course, I didn't. Why would I have money? "Why?" I asked. "Because I spent all my money on popcorn and candy. I don't have any money for the train."

Well, where could we find some money? I didn't know a soul in Chicago. Then I had a revelation. Several years ago, when I was about fourteen, my aunt Sadie treated me to a day downtown. We had lunch and she took me to a movie. At the movie theater, she introduced me to her friend who was a ticket taker. He was a little old man who looked very distinguished in his ticket-taker uniform. She said, "Alice, this is my friend, Louie. You can call him Uncle Louie." I said my "how do you do" and he and Aunt Sadie talked for a while before we went into the movie.

"George! I do know someone in Chicago! He works at one of these big theaters. He might loan us some money." So we ran around to several theaters until I spied a little old man who was a ticket taker. "There he is! Uncle Louie! Do you remember me? I'm Aunt Sadie's niece, Alice. Uncle Louie, we're in a lot of trouble. You see, George spent all his money on candy and popcorn, and now we don't have any money to take the train home. Could we borrow some money? I promise I'll pay you back next Saturday."

The little old man listened to my story with great concern, then smiled and reached in his pocket and handed me a five-dollar bill. "Oh, Uncle Louie! Thank you so much! I love you." And after giving him a big hug and a kiss on his wrinkled cheek, George and I dashed off to catch the last train.

The next day was Sunday. As usual, Aunt Sadie and Aunt Tony came to our house for Sunday dinner. I started telling Aunt Sadie about our predicament the night before. When I got to the part where George had spent all his money, my mother rolled her eyes heavenward. This sort of irresponsibility confirmed her dislike for That Crazy George.

I continued with my story, telling Aunt Sadie, "And guess what? I went to the Rialto and found Uncle Louie and he gave us the money to get home!" How proud I was that I had remembered her friend!

Aunt Sadie looked at me with a puzzled expression and said, "Louie doesn't work at the Rialto. He works at the Oriental!"

So the following Saturday, I took the train to downtown Chicago, found the kind stranger, and returned his five dollars.

Young love

Listening to Big Band records

Sixteen

Tennis, anyone?

5

Don't Speak to Strangers

G RADUATION DAY, JUNE 3, 1943, was joyful and a bit sad as we said good-bye to many of the boys who were entering the armed services. There were almost five hundred graduates in our class.

In the early 1940s, parents who could afford it sent their sons to college. Girls were expected to marry, have children, and make a comfortable home for their family.

I knew there were no savings for my college education, but I had taken college preparatory courses and some secretarial courses—shorthand, typing, bookkeeping. My plan was to work until I saved enough to pay for college myself.

My boyfriend, George, was exempt from military service, so he went away to college in the fall. I started to work in downtown Chicago as secretary to the claims manager of Continental Casualty Insurance. My boss was very nice. He had two sons in the army, and he worried about them and talked with me about them. I found new friends among the girls who worked in the building.

My social life continued as it had during high school although there weren't as many boys. There were still many former high school friends in the area, and we went to movies, dances, bowling, swimming, and hiking. Summer vacations and Christmas breaks were reserved for spending time with George.

In June 1944, I had the opportunity to travel to California with a friend. My friend, Betty, had just completed her first year at Principia College, and during the year she was there, her family moved from Park Ridge to San Francisco. Betty was to join them when her summer vacation began. Betty's father purchased two train tickets, so she would have both seats to herself and wouldn't run the risk of having to share it with a stranger. Trains were crowded in those days as servicemen were traveling across the country to get to their duty stations or going home on leave. Betty's father was being protective of his young daughter who would be traveling alone for three days and three nights.

Betty invited me to use the extra seat on the train. All I had to pay for was my return train trip. I jumped at the opportunity. I had an aunt (my father's sister) in Los Angeles that I had never met, so I planned to go there by train after a few days in San Francisco.

My parents and my sister bid good-bye to us at the train station in Chicago and admonished us not to talk with strangers, especially servicemen. We promised and climbed on board. It was evening and the seats had already been converted to sleeping berths. Betty had the upper berth. I had the lower one.

The next morning while we were having breakfast in the dining car, a soldier at the next table was telling his table mates that he had to stand up all night as he didn't have a seat, and even the lounge car was full of soldiers sleeping. He said he had been home on leave and had to get to San Francisco on this train because he was "shipping out" in one week.

Betty and I had a wonderful idea. We would share her upper berth, and I would offer the soldier my berth. In keeping with my promise not to talk with servicemen, I wrote a note and gave it to the waiter to deliver it. The note read, "Would you like to sleep in my berth tonight?"

He opened the note, looked over at me, and sprung to his feet. Standing by our table, he asked, "Did you send this note?" I nodded. He asked, "Do you mean it?" I answered, "Yes." He said, "Wow, that's great!" I said demurely, "Oh, it's my patriotic duty." And I gave him the number of my sleeping berth. "Can I buy you a drink or something?" I told him not to feel obligated and I didn't drink anyway. "See you tonight, then," he said.

That night, on my way back from brushing my teeth in the ladies' room, I started to climb up into Betty's berth. A hand reached out and grabbed my leg. "Hi. Isn't this your berth?" It was the serviceman. I told him it was. "Well, where are you going? Why are you climbing up there?" I told him I was going to sleep with Betty. "But aren't you going to sleep down here?"

"Of course not! What made you think that?" He showed me the note I had written and I could see how he misinterpreted it. "I knew it was too good to be true," he said.

We arrived safely in San Francisco. Betty's father met us at the train and asked us about the trip. We omitted the part about the serviceman. I stayed at Betty's house for about five days, and Betty's parents took us sightseeing. We went to the top of the Mark, had dinner in Chinatown where I tried fried shrimp for the first time and loved it, and rode the trolleys up and down the steep hills.

During this time in June 1944, the allies launched the Normandy invasion, and our hopes were raised for an end to the war. It was not to become a reality for another year.

I bid Betty and her parents good-bye when I boarded the train for Los Angeles. There, my aunt Elsie and her husband met me. Aunt Elsie was a very eccentric woman and was so happy to have a young niece visit her. She had all kinds of plans for me. Her husband, Uncle Dave, was a frail-looking man, although he was only in his early fifties at that time. He had been born and raised in the South and was a true Southern gentleman. He wore white suits and was lovingly devoted to my aunt.

They lived in Hollywood. Aunt Elsie had been a hairdresser for the movie stars during the silent movie days. She talked about Mary Pickford and Marie Dressler who had been very popular, but the names were unfamiliar to me. One day, she took me to one of the movie star's home. It was a mansion set on spacious grounds with a high fence and gate.

We were welcomed in and led up a large circular stairway to the boudoir of her friend. The retired movie star was sitting at her dressing table and took my hand when we were introduced. She showed me all around her huge bedroom. She had a walk-in closet that was larger than my bedroom at home. It was filled with beautiful clothes. I noticed everything was white and gold. The woodwork and doors were white instead of the oak and mahogany back home. It felt like a fairy princess's house.

One morning, Aunt Elsie took me to her bank. She went to her safe deposit box and showed me some things in it. One box held a beautiful diamond dinner ring. "I'm going to leave that to you when I'm gone, Alice." she said. I have that ring now and have worn it many times. Aunt Elsie never had any children. She left a diamond ring to my sister also.

Her next-door neighbors had a daughter about my age, and they arranged for us to have a day together. I can't remember her name, but she was very interesting and told me about some child stars she had known. That night, we went to a large ballroom where one of the big bands was playing. A man who looked exactly like Gene Kelley asked me to dance. He was an excellent dancer and had a great personality. I asked him if he knew he looked like Gene Kelley and he said, "Well, I should. I'm his stand-in!" I was not sure I believed that. It would have been easier for me to believe him if he said he was Gene Kelley because he had all the mannerisms and facial expressions.

Aunt Elsie shampooed my hair while I was at her house. As she was rinsing my hair, she said, "Always use cool water for the final rinse. It makes the hair look so nice." I think of Aunt Elsie every time I rinse my hair.

My train trip home was the southern route. We skirted the desert, and as we headed for Texas, the experienced travelers warned us to put wet washcloths on our faces. There was no air conditioning on the train, and we were told it was unbearably hot in Texas. I braced for the heat wave, but didn't really feel it was so bad. I arrived safely in Chicago with much to tell my friends and family.

I continued working for the insurance company, saving what I could toward college. One day in April 1945 as I was riding home on the train after work, I heard people talking in hushed tones. I looked around to see many different reactions on people's faces. Some of them were crying. Others looked shocked. "What happened?" I asked.

"President Roosevelt is dead" was the answer. I sat there in disbelief. President Roosevelt had been in office most of my life. I was seven years old in January 1933 when he took office and guided us through the Depression. Now I was nineteen. He was the only president I had ever known.

Important events followed quickly. On May 7, V-E Day, the war in Europe ended. We celebrated and looked to the East for an end to that war. On August 6, the United States dropped an atomic bomb on the city of Hiroshima in Japan. When we saw the newsreels in the movie theaters, we were horrified to see the mass destruction and the great loss of lives. On August 14, Japan surrendered, and we were told the atomic bomb had saved the loss of many more lives. On September 2, the Japanese signed the terms of surrender and war was officially over.

The advent of the atomic bomb caused a panic that lasted for decades. There was fear that the next war would be an atomic war and all the nations would be annihilated.

Russia, who had been our ally, was soon to become our enemy, and the two great nations would enter into several decades of suspicion and distrust. It was called the Cold War.

September of 1945 came and I still didn't have enough money saved for college. Then I heard about Blackburn College in southern Illinois that was within my reach financially.

All the students worked two hours a day at various jobs on the campus. The work hours were credited toward tuition, dormitory, and meals. I went to Carlinville and talked with the admissions officer and the head of the English Department. I decided I would start the following September 1946. Now I had a definite goal and my future was becoming a reality.

George and I had a mutual birthday. On July 13, 1946, we celebrated together and had a long heart-to-heart talk. I was looking forward to leaving for college in six weeks. I would make new friends and develop new interests. George and I had shared many good times and had affection for each other, but as we were growing up, we were also growing apart. The time had come for each of us to pursue our own dreams. We parted cheerfully and kept in touch regularly. And so ended a chapter in my life.

Modeling one of Aunt Elsie's costumes

6

A Chapter Ends. My Future Begins.

IN SIX WEEKS, my dream would come true. Nothing could alter my course now.

I corresponded with my future roommate, and we planned the color scheme for our room: curtains, bedspreads, and other accessories. I was still working for Mr. Weiler at the insurance office. The war had ended, and his sons were home safe and sound.

Our private office was moved to another floor in the building, and I found myself in a large open office with about ten other men and women. Mr. Weiler had a small private office where I would enter when he wanted to dictate letters, but I returned to my desk in the large office to do my work.

I started to notice little gifts on my desk when I came back from lunch and coffee breaks. Sometimes it was a small box of raisins. Other times, it was a candy bar or cookies. I couldn't guess who was doing this, but one day I came back earlier than usual and caught the culprit. It was Byron, the man who had the desk in back of me.

He was a rather quiet man—good-looking with black wavy hair and deep brown eyes. He had been an Air Force officer and was discharged in November 1945 after the war ended. During the war, he and several buddies planned to open a business in Chicago. When the war ended, Byron went to Chicago to meet his friends, but they had all decided to stay in their own hometowns. So Byron stayed in Chicago and took a job as an insurance adjuster, and that is how he happened to be in the desk behind me.

We started talking, and before long, he asked me for a date. I hesitated because I really didn't know anything about him, and he was ten years older than me. I had always dated boys from my hometown and high school.

I invited him to dinner at my house instead of going out with him. I met him at the train station on a Sunday afternoon, and we walked the mile to my home for my mother's Sunday dinner. My family liked him immediately. We went for a walk after dinner, and I showed him our small town. The next time he asked me for a date, I accepted.

And now, a very important chapter in my life is about to begin.

Working Girl

7

First Date—A Disaster

BYRON ASKED ME where I'd like to go on our first date. I told him I'd like to see the ballet at the Chicago Civic Opera House. He bought the tickets for the following night and said he would take me out to dinner after work and we would go to the ballet afterward.

The next morning, I spent so much time deciding what to wear, I didn't have time for breakfast. I just barely made it to the train station in time to catch the train to Chicago.

During my lunch hour, I decided my clothes didn't look sophisticated enough for a date with an older man, so I skipped lunch and spent the hour shopping for a black dress—my first black dress.

Five o'clock came. I changed into my black dress, and Byron and I walked down Michigan Boulevard. We came to a cocktail lounge and Byron suggested we stop in there. I agreed, thinking it was a restaurant and assumed we were going to eat dinner there.

When we entered and were ushered to a table, I noticed the premises were not very well lit and the table was so small I didn't know how they could serve two dinners on it. I had just turned twenty-one, but I was very immature and unsophisticated. I had never been in a cocktail lounge and I had never had an alcoholic drink.

When the waiter asked for our orders, I wondered why he didn't give us a menu. I just gave Byron a puzzled look and Byron ordered two martinis.

That's when I realized I was going to have my first drink. *Well, okay*, I thought to myself. *I can handle this. There's always a first time.* The waiter brought the drinks. *This won't be so bad*, I thought. It was a small glass with an olive in it. I love olives.

I was accustomed to guzzling down soft drinks and I was rather thirsty and hungry. After all, I hadn't eaten since yesterday!

So I picked up the glass and, with all the affected worldliness I could muster, drank the contents in a few gulps. I remember the dim lights getting dimmer and then nothing. Far away, I could hear someone saying, "Alice! Alice! Wake up. Are you all right? I've got to get you out of here. Can you stand up?"

I became aware that someone was trying to put my jacket on me, but my arms felt like spaghetti. My hat had fallen off. (All ladies wore hats in the 1940s. Look at the old movies, you'll see.) Byron plopped it on my head at a jaunty angle. I felt myself being lifted up and carefully walked to the door.

We were outside, a fresh breeze was wafting in from Lake Michigan and I was walking on the sides of my high-heeled shoes. Byron held on to me with one hand under my arm and the other arm around my waist. We walked for quite a while, and by the time we arrived at the Palmer House where Byron had dinner reservations, I had regained a degree of decorum.

This was Chicago's most famous hotel and restaurant. Byron checked his hat with the hat check girl. (All men in the 1940s wore hats.) We started to walk up the red carpeted stairs when I felt something snap.

Now I have to explain what silk stockings and garter belts were. In the 1940s, panty hose had not yet been invented. Women wore long sheer silk stockings that came up to the thighs. They were held up by a garter belt we wore around our waist and it had elastic garter hooks, one in the front and one in the back for each stocking.

I already knew one of the back garters had broken off several weeks ago, but I never got around to sewing it back on. The front garter was doing a good job of holding my stocking up.

Well, when I felt the snap, I realized the front garter had been stressed too much from being the sole support of my stocking and it took that very moment to break and cause a downward descent of my stocking. Each step I took up the stairs caused my stocking to sink lower. I tried walking with my knees tight together, but when I reached the last stair, the stocking was well on its way past my knee and down to my ankle. As the head waiter told us to follow him, my stocking had folded over my shoe and was trailing along in back of me with the broken garter still attached to it.

Apparently, Byron was unaware of the drama that was going on. He was looking ahead at the waiter and not down at the floor. There was a lovely string orchestra playing soft romantic music as I passed tables full of people, my stocking dragging behind me.

During dinner, Byron told me about his family in Manchester, New Hampshire, and showed me pictures of his mother and father, sister and brothers. While he was busy talking, I was busily pulling up my stocking and desperately trying to think of a way to attach it to something.

This wasn't a genuine silk stocking. Silk stockings were made in Japan, and we had been fighting Japan for four years so there were no real silk stockings available for American women. We had to be satisfied with rayon stockings. Nylon was not yet on the market. Rayon was a poor substitute for silk because it had no resiliency. Once it had been stretched, it stayed stretched and didn't snap back. Since the thigh is larger than the calf, this stocking was not going to stay up without some help.

I decided to stretch the top of the stocking even further by trying to tie a knot in the excess upper part, thus making the stocking tight around my thigh. I succeeded in doing this under the table while pretending to listen to Byron. When it was time to leave for the ballet, we stood up, and immediately, the knot untied and the wayward stocking succeeded in its mission to fall over my shoe and embarrass me in front of everyone. I made my way to the ladies' room where the attendant gave me a safety pin. She held out her hand for a tip, but I had no money with me. I had spent it all on a black dress. So I shook her hand and thanked her.

Byron had a taxi waiting for us and when I got in I was still embarrassed and felt the evening was a failure. I told Byron I wasn't feeling well and just wanted to go home. I thought he would just take me to the train station, but he told the taxi driver to take us to Park Ridge, a forty-minute drive.

As we rode in the taxi, I reflected on how stupid I had been for trying to make an impression, trying to act sophisticated and worldly. While these thoughts went through my head, Byron put his arm around me and said, "Alice, do you know what I like about you?" I couldn't imagine there was anything to like about me after this evening's debacle. I shrugged listlessly. He said, "You don't try to be someone you're not."

The next morning I just didn't want to go to the office and face Byron, so I called in sick. About 10:00 a.m., the doorbell rang. My mother went to the door and came to my room with a box of a dozen red roses and a card that read, "Sorry you are sick. I hope you are better soon. Love, By."

My mother was ecstatic. "Now THAT's the kind of man you should marry—not one of these kids you hang around with."

"Mom," I said wearily, "He's too old for me. I'm out of my league with him." Mom dispensed a thought from her store of wise sayings. "Well, it's better to be an old man's darling than a young man's slave." I don't know the source of my mother's many wise sayings. I disregarded some of them, but some of them made good sense. This one was way off base. I was NOT going to be any old man's darling!

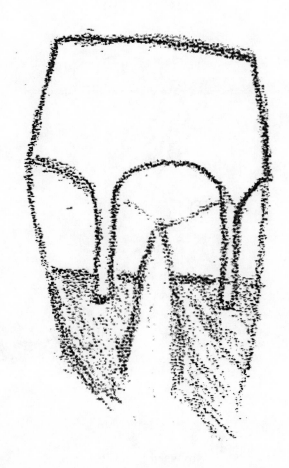

Garter Belt

Wayward Stocking

8

My Dream—At Last!

BYRON ASKED ME for another date, much to my surprise. For the next three weeks, we dated steadily and learned more about each other. I found myself looking forward to our times together.

He had graduated from Ohio State University in 1939 with a major in business and a minor in geography. During his four years at Ohio State, he dated a girl. They planned to get married, but broke up shortly before graduation.

Byron went back to his hometown in Manchester, New Hampshire, and went to work for the Remington Rand Corporation, a business machine company. Europe was in turmoil as Hitler rose to power and Germany invaded Poland. Although the United States was not yet involved in Europe's troubles, the Selective Service Act was signed in 1940, and in 1941, young men were being drafted to serve in the army.

Byron decided to enlist, and in April 1941, he was stationed at Hickham Field, Hawaii. He was an intelligence research analyst. One Sunday morning, December 7, 1941, he left the building where he had eaten breakfast and was walking across the square toward his barracks when bombs started exploding all around him. The sky was filled with planes. People on the ground were running helter-skelter. Byron saw friends who were running toward him get hit by the explosions.

It was a long day of chaos. Byron joined other men who tried to open the storage buildings where ammunition was kept, but the buildings were locked and they couldn't get in. Our planes couldn't get off the ground, and many were blown apart on the airstrip.

That night, he sat on the grass and watched the ships burning far below in Pearl Harbor.

He spent the next four years in the Pacific area as an intelligence officer and was discharged at the end of the war as a captain in the United States Army Air Force.

Each day brought me closer to my departure for Blackburn College. Each date with Byron became special. I sensed that this friendship could become more serious. On our last date, Byron asked me to reconsider and stay. I knew he was going to propose marriage, and I interrupted him before he got to that point. I told him I had been planning and saving for a long time and I was determined to go.

So off to Blackburn I went. During orientation week, I knew I had made the right choice. I made new friends, had new experiences, and my roommate was delightful. I was eager to start classes. Although I was almost three years older than most of the girls, the freshman boys were my age or older. Their education had been delayed because they had been in the armed services.

My first letter from Byron brought a tug to my heart, but I shrugged it off. This is where I belonged.

Dormitory life was a new experience for me. At that time, there were separate dormitories for men and for women. Men were not allowed beyond the reception room in the women's dormitory. Our dormitory had a housemother who kept track of our coming in and going out. There was also a curfew at night. On weeknights, we had to be in by 9:00 p.m. On Friday and Saturday nights, we were allowed to stay out until 11:00 p.m. We had to sign our names in a book when we left and when we came back. The doors were locked at curfew time. There were a few times I was late getting back. Luckily, the fire escape led up to my dormitory room on the second floor and my roommate let me in through the window. I wasn't accustomed to such strict rules. It had been years since I had a curfew at home.

I did love living in a dormitory, in spite of the restrictions. It was like having a building full of sisters. We all became close friends and loaned and borrowed clothes and jewelry from each other. There was always someone to talk with.

Every Saturday morning, there was room inspection. Our rooms had to be cleaned and dusted. Clothes had to be folded in our drawers or hung neatly in our closets. If we didn't pass inspection, we had to stay in our room until it did pass inspection. Needless to say, my roommate and I spent the morning cleaning up our messy room so we could have the afternoon free.

The town was only a mile from the campus, and on Saturday afternoons, after room inspection, some of my girl friends and I walked into town to get ice cream or soft drinks at the soda fountain. There was a movie theater that we could go to also.

My classes were small. There were no large lecture halls. I had expected more in-depth studies. My first work assignment was to clean the chapel. I spent two hours every morning dusting and sweeping. On my first day at this job, a very handsome young man stopped by to talk with me while I dusted. I remembered meeting him at an orientation picnic. He was back from the war. He was a local boy and he was my age. We started dating.

When I went home during Christmas break, Byron and I were together almost every evening. I had never been away from home for more than two weeks before, and I realized how much I missed my family. I appreciated the joyful family gatherings and my mother's good food. Byron met many of my relatives and felt at ease with them. Celebrating Christmas and welcoming the New Year in the warmth of my home and family with Byron beside me, I realized I was falling in love with him. It was very hard to return to Blackburn in January.

My classes ceased to hold my interest and my thoughts drifted back to the good times Byron and I had over the Christmas holidays. In February, we had a midwinter break and I hurried back home. As soon as I got in the door, I called Byron at his office, and we arranged to meet in downtown Chicago that night.

We went to a night club that had recently opened. After we were seated at a table, a girl came up to us with a tray of flower corsages. Byron bought a corsage for me and pinned it on me. When the waiter asked what I would have to drink, I said, "Red wine and soda." That was the popular drink among the Blackburn crowd. The waiter looked shocked and disgusted. "Did you say wine and soda?" Byron stared him down and stated, "The lady wants wine and soda."

The band started to play and I took one sip of my drink when Byron said, "Let's get out of here."

"But we just got here and you'll have to pay the cover charge anyway," I said. He insisted, so we left the night club and started walking when Byron suddenly stopped, took me by the shoulders, and said, "You're going to marry me! I'm not taking no for an answer." I looked into his eyes and saw the determination and sincerity. It was a moment that swirled around and landed in my heart with the declaration of truth. Yes! This is where I really belong! This is my destiny! I found my voice and answered, "Yes, I'll marry you."

We kissed and embraced and cried, right there on that street in Chicago. There was a drugstore nearby and we went in and ordered ice cream sodas to celebrate.

9

The Wedding

T HE NEXT DAY was Saturday. Byron came to my house that afternoon with an engagement ring and we were officially engaged. He said he had seen that ring in the display window of a jewelry store every day as he walked to work, hoping for the day he would purchase it.

We were married in April. I didn't return to Blackburn. There were too many things to do before the wedding. The wedding was at home in front of the fireplace, just like my sister's wedding. My mother had new carpeting installed, and all the aunts came over to clean and polish everything the day before the wedding. Aunt Sadie made a beautiful wedding cake.

My cousin, Shirley, was my maid of honor. On the night of the wedding, we were upstairs in my bedroom, happily talking and waiting for the wedding march music to start. When we heard the music, Shirley started down the stairs. I had a brief moment of panic and turned back toward the bedroom. Shirley looked back and hissed, "Alice!" I looked at her blankly.

Shirley took another step down. I whispered, "Is Byron down there?" She had just reached the turn where she was able to see the fireplace and Byron and the pastor. She looked back at me, smiled, winked, and nodded her head. My fear dissipated immediately, and I took my first step down the stairs. My father was waiting by the bottom step. Byron was smiling at me as I descended. The living room and dining room were filled with loving relatives and friends, all smiling. Flowers were everywhere, on the banisters of the staircase, in front of the fireplace, and on the mantle. I was surrounded with love.

Pastor Spangler performed the ceremony with over one hundred people attending. I sneaked a look at my mother during the ceremony to see if she was crying like she did at my sister's wedding, but she was smiling.

When it was time for Byron and me to leave for our honeymoon, I changed into my new trousseau clothes—a fitted gray suit, pink blouse, and a fluffy pink hat. My mother apparently just realized she had never told me about the facts of life, so she sent a recently married cousin to my room to tell me what to expect.

Marian wasn't exactly sure what my mother wanted her to tell me, so while I was combing my hair and putting on lipstick, she said, "Your mom wants me to tell you about married life." I looked at her with mild interest. Marian continued, "Well, all I can think of is it took me a long time to figure out how long to cook the potatoes so they were done by the time the meat was cooked."

I looked at her with amazement. I had no idea what she was talking about, but I thanked her and left the room prepared for married life. Byron and I bid everyone good-bye amid showers of rice and a real April rain shower.

We arrived at the Edgewater Beach Hotel where Byron told the clerk he had reserved the honeymoon suite. As I looked down to watch him sign the register, rice fell out of my fluffy pink hat onto the counter. My happy new life had begun.

Rice Showers and Rain Showers

We went to New Hampshire on our honeymoon and visited Byron's family. His mother and father couldn't come to the wedding because his mother was ill. We flew from Chicago to Boston and took a train from Boston to Manchester, New Hampshire.

The train pulled into the station at Manchester. I was a little nervous about meeting his family. Dressed in my gray suit and fluffy pink hat, I stepped down from the train and my high heel was caught in the mesh of the steel step. I walked right out of my shoe. So much for a dignified entrance! I started to laugh while I slipped my shoe back on, and a very distinguished-looking white-haired gentleman walked toward us smiling. Byron introduced his father. His father said, "I knew you were the right girl for my son the minute I saw you." That put me at ease and endeared him forever in my heart.

We drove up to a large Victorian-style house and climbed the stairs to the front porch (or *piazza* as they call it in New England). Byron's mother opened the door, gave Byron a big hug, then took one look at me, and said, "I could never wear a hat like that!" I didn't quite know how to react to that.

Byron's sister was standing behind her mother. She was two years younger than me and she smiled and welcomed me. Soon Byron's two brothers and their wives came to the house to meet me and I liked them immediately.

We stayed with his folks a few days and then borrowed his father's car to drive up to the White Mountains. We stayed in cabins in the woods. This was before there were motels. Some of the cabins were very rustic, but we didn't mind. One day, as we drove through a small town, Byron stopped at a hardware store and told me to wait in the car. He said he was going to buy me a present. He came out with a .22 rifle. "That's my present?" I asked. He said, "I'm going to teach you how to shoot at targets."

When we got to some thick woods, we got out and looked for tin cans. Byron lined them up on a rock and proceeded to show me how to aim and shoot at the cans. He knocked a few of the cans over with his shots. Then he handed it to me with more instructions. I took aim and shot each of the cans off the rock. I admitted to him later that I had learned target shooting at a YMCA camp when I was nine years old and I got pretty good at it.

We came south from the mountains to pay a visit to Byron's Aunt Harriet and Uncle Charles in Portsmouth. It was a quaint town with old narrow streets. Aunt Harriet was much friendlier than Byron's mother and I liked her immediately. They took us to a lovely place for dinner and drove us to the shore so I could have my first sight of the magnificent Atlantic Ocean. I could have watched those crashing waves for hours.

I fell in love with New Hampshire and its majestic mountains, woodlands, and brooks. It was so different from the flatlands and endless cornfields in Illinois. I asked Byron if we could stay in New Hampshire. He arranged a transfer to the Boston office and went back to Chicago to pack our things.

10

First Home

WHILE BYRON WAS back in Chicago, I stayed with his parents. His sister Doie (short for Eudora) and I became good friends. His mother remained aloof. His father did everything in his power to make me feel at home. I realized later that his mother was extremely hard of hearing. In those days, hearing aids were very inefficient. She wore a large battery that was pinned on her dress with a wire running up to a device in her ear. The only voices she could understand were her husband's and Doie's. She couldn't pick up my voice at all.

Byron was transferred to the Boston office and commuted by train. We started hunting for a place to live. His brother, George, was also looking for a house. He and his wife had four small children and the house they were renting had been sold so they had to vacate.

We lived with his parents while we searched for a house. I quickly learned that living in my mother-in-law's house was very different from living in my parents' house. While Byron was in Boston all day, I tried to be helpful around the house, but my housekeeping skills were limited and my cooking skills were nonexistent. I made our bed every day, kept our clothes hung up, and wiped dishes after meals. But Mrs. Worthen was definitely the boss of that house and things had to be done her way.

She was extremely upset when she found out I had washed my nylon stockings in the bathroom sink and hung them to dry on the shower rod.

That just isn't done in her house. I didn't understand what all the fuss was about. My mother never complained when I did it at home.

One morning, I decided I was going to make the dessert for the evening meal. I walked to the little grocery store a few blocks away and bought a box of cherry Jell-O. After carefully reading the instructions on the box, I went to work boiling water and choosing a bowl. Byron's mother came into the kitchen to see what I was doing. Then she phoned her husband at work and told him to bring home two quarts of fresh strawberries and a bottle of whipping cream.

She made a two-layer strawberry shortcake with juicy strawberries oozing out from the layers. The whole thing was topped high with whipped cream. When Byron came home, I told him I made Jell-O for dessert. When we finished supper, I went to the refrigerator and proudly brought forth the Jell-O. Byron's mother appeared with her masterpiece strawberry shortcake. After cutting a huge piece and sliding it onto a plate, she held it aloft and said, "Byron?"

I held my breath. I couldn't look up. Then Byron said, "No thanks, Mom. I just *love* cherry Jell-O." I have never doubted his love since then.

We found a house that had two large apartments: one upstairs and one downstairs. Byron's family asked us to buy that house so George and his family would have a place to live. So we bought the house, and we took the upstairs apartment. George's wife, Shirley, was very nice and fun to be with. We became good friends.

Our first baby, Patricia Joan, was born followed a year later by Byron Stevens Worthen Jr. (Buz). Two years later, Kenneth Gordon Worthen arrived. It was a busy household.

Barbara Sue didn't make her entrance until five years later. You will meet these characters throughout the book.

I truly believe children are born with certain traits already in place, and although they grow up in the same family environment, each of them will become the individual they are destined to be. It is fascinating to watch their inborn traits develop from babyhood to adulthood. Each child has a unique personality and each is loved for his/her own individuality.

Patty was a very independent little girl who grew up to be a capable, independent woman. Buz had an insatiable curiosity and a delightful sense of humor. Ken was a quiet boy who showed early signs of leadership and generosity. Barbara had a creative imagination and a tender, loving heart. They all have their own very interesting life stories, and I hope they share them with their children some day.

11

Patty's Oil Bath

WHEN OUR FIRST child, Patricia Joan Worthen, was born, mothers and babies were kept in the hospital for a week to ten days. I wasn't allowed to get out of bed for two days. On the third day after Patty was born, I was allowed to dangle my legs on the side of the bed for a few minutes. By the time they finally let me stand up a few days later, I was so weak I had to hold on to the nurse to keep from falling. During this period of confinement, I was given bed baths and back rubs. Patty was brought to me at four-hour intervals. The food was actually delicious, and I felt like I was residing in a beauty spa.

The doctor who had been following me along during my pregnancy and delivered the baby charged $75. This included all the prenatal visits, delivery, and one year of follow-up and injections for the baby.

Things had changed by the time Barbara Sue was born. She was born in the hospital at West Point Academy. When I was wheeled from the delivery room to a hospital bed, I was told to get up and walk to the bathroom by myself. Also, I was to walk down the hall to bring my baby back to the room when it was feeding time. I left the hospital with Barbara in three days and hadn't lost any strength at all.

The time had come to bring our first baby home. Being the youngest in my family, I knew nothing about taking care of babies. I had done some babysitting during my teen years, but the children I took care of were five or six years old.

I watched as the nurse showed me how to fold a diaper and the proper way to pin it. There were no disposable diapers at that time. All diapers were cloth and had to be washed, dried, and folded.

The doctor came in the room with instructions about feeding the baby. I was breast-feeding Patty. The doctor said I should feed her every four hours, and if she cried before the four hours were up, I was to just let her cry.

The last instruction he gave me was that the first bath should be an oil bath. He didn't explain that he meant I should saturate a cotton ball with baby oil and rub her body with it.

So when we arrived home I checked my stock of baby oil. I had two large bottles that were given to me at a baby shower. That really wasn't going to be enough to fill the Bathinette, so I sent Byron out for several more bottles of baby oil. The following day, as Byron was at work and I was alone with our precious child, I decided it was time to give her the first bath. I emptied all the bottles of baby oil into the Bathinette and lowered Patty carefully into it. Suddenly, I was groping to keep hold of my baby. She kept slipping out of my hands. I tried to take her out of the tub, but she slid right back in. Panic gripped me. I was never going to get her out of there and she would drown! I tried scooping her up the side of the tub. I almost succeeded, but at the last minute, she slipped back in. By that time, my heart was racing, beads of perspiration were dripping from my forehead, and my hair felt like it was standing out straight.

I tried the scooping technique again, and this time I succeeded. I wrapped her up in a blanket, thanked God for his intervention, and Patty and I settled down for a long nap.

I had a lot to learn and I wanted to do everything right. I bought a book with instructions on bathing, feeding, and toilet training a baby. Even the baby book said the baby should be fed every four hours, not a minute earlier.

Patty, of course, had never read that book and demanded to be fed when she was hungry.

I called my mother-in-law in desperation once while Patty cried lustily. It was only three hours since her last feeding. "What should I do?" I asked. Byron's mother said, "Make her wait. Don't give in. She'll run your life if you give in to her!"

Byron came home from work to find me worn out and upset while Patty continued to cry.

"What's wrong?" he asked. I explained that I still had to wait fifteen minutes before I could feed the baby. "Why not feed her now?"

"Because the doctor and the book say every four hours. Even your mother said I have to wait."

Byron put his arm around me, and in gentle tones, while the baby screamed, he said, "Alice, you are a woman. You are as much a woman as my mother and your mother. You can choose to do what you want with your own child. Make your own rules. Go, feed the baby. She's hungry."

I found my confidence that day. No babies of mine would have to wait four hours to be fed if they were hungry. And it turned out to be all right. None of my children tried to run my life!

12

A Fork in the Road a Decision

BYRON WORKED FOR Continental Insurance Company in Boston for about a year after we bought the house in Manchester, New Hampshire. It was a long commute by train, and he had been thinking about becoming an independent insurance broker with an office in Manchester. He explained that we would be living on commissions instead of a steady salary.

I told him to go ahead and do it. He could always go back to a salaried position if it didn't work out. He tried very hard. I did his secretarial work. He sold a few policies and we rejoiced, but then weeks went by before he sold any more. It was feast or famine. Bills started to pile up and we were sinking into debt.

Kenneth Gordon Worthen was born on October 4, 1950. Now we had three young children and the insurance business was not doing well. Byron was starting to look into joining an established insurance firm with a guaranteed salary.

The Korean War broke out and reserve officers were being recalled to serve in the military. Byron was in the reserves, and he received a notice that he was recalled.

We talked it over. "I could be exempt. I'm married and have three children," he said.

"But would you want to go back in the service?" I asked. I already knew the answer to that. He looked forward to the reserve meetings. He was much more interested in the world affairs than he was in insurance. "If I went back in, I might as well make a career out of it. That would mean fifteen or twenty years of traveling and living in different places."

The idea of new places and traveling appealed to me. I had lived in Park Ridge, Illinois, all my life. I felt adventurous. "I wouldn't mind traveling," I said.

We had come to the fork in the road. One way was safe, sure, settled. We would remain in Manchester, and Byron would continue in the insurance business on a salary instead of commissions. The other way was interesting, unknown. Byron would return to something he loved. He had the capacity to work for something he was keenly interested in and he would be serving his country.

He made the right decision.

13

Where the Eedies Lived

T HE FIRST ASSIGNMENT my husband had when he was recalled to active duty was at a radar station in Brunswick, Maine. He went there first and found a house for us to rent, and we followed a few weeks later. The house was in the country on a peninsula in an area called Harpswell. There was a small general store across the road, a two-room schoolhouse down the road, and a community church. Two or three houses were within walking distance.

Our house had a name. It was called Guernsey Villa. In the days of horse-and-buggy, it was used as a country hotel where wealthy families spent the summer while the husbands stayed in the cities to work. The husbands came to Brunswick by train and were met with a horse-and-buggy that took them to Guernsey Villa to spend weekends with their wives and children.

There were many bedrooms on the second floor. Each one had a fireplace and large windows. The main floor had many rooms besides the dining room, kitchen, and bathroom. They probably had been used for card playing, reading, and other activities.

There was a large enclosed porch that covered the entire side of the house that had been used as a breakfast room. It was lovely, with a beautiful hardwood floor and connecting windows on the outside wall that afforded a view of the countryside and allowed the sun to brighten the breakfast tables.

This house was rented to us for $30 a month. It had been repossessed by the bank from the latest owners for nonpayment of the mortgage and was being offered for sale for $2,000. Unfortunately, we were not in a financial position at that time to assume a $2,000 debt, but what a wonderful vacation house that could have been!

Since there were so many rooms on the first floor, we didn't need the upstairs rooms. We limited our living space to the main floor and closed the door leading to the second floor to conserve heat during the winter.

We arrived at Guernsey Villa in the spring of 1951. It was a lovely time. Daffodils were blooming in the garden by the enclosed porch. We had ocean on three sides. In June, when we took walks to the rocky shores, we picked wild blueberries on the way. We quickly made friends with the Palmers who owned the general store. They had a large, happy family. Patty and Buz called Mr. and Mrs. Palmer "Bampa" and "Bama." They were given small treats every time we visited the store. Two of their teenage daughters became reliable babysitters for the few times we went to Brunswick for a movie.

One of their daughters, Irene, was married and lived nearby. She had four small children. We soon became good friends and remain so to this day. We spent many days taking the children to the shore with a picnic lunch, watching them run freely around the sand and rocks.

The long summer stretched into September, and by October, the New England autumn presented landscapes that rivaled famous paintings. There was a chill in the air and the skies held a promise of snow.

On cold rainy days, I opened up the upstairs rooms and the children could run around playing hide-and-seek while I hung my laundry in the attic room. Kenny was just twelve months old and disposable diapers had not yet been invented. I washed diapers and clothes every day, and I didn't have a clothes dryer so I rigged up a clothesline in the attic for inclement days.

One night in October, Patty woke up crying. She and Buz shared a room. I went to her and asked her what was wrong. She said, "The Eedies!"

"What about the Eedies?" I asked.

"The Eedies are coming!"

"What is an Eedie?" I asked.

She shrugged, "I don't know."

Buz started to whimper about the Eedies so I tried to calm him. Kenny was in the adjoining room and started crying just because the others were crying.

"Where are the Eedies? Are they in the closet?"

They shook their heads no.

"Are they under the bed?"

The answer was no.

"Well, then, where are the Eedies?"

Their eyes were wide with fright as they pointed their little fingers to the ceiling. "Upstairs?" I asked. They nodded and both of them wailed. Kenny wailed from his crib. I gathered them all up and brought them into our bed.

"What's the matter?" Byron asked.

"The Eedies are after them" I explained.

The next day was cold and rainy. I started up the stairs with my wet laundry and called the children to join me. They refused, whimpering something about the Eedies. So I waited until their nap time to hang the laundry upstairs.

That night, Patty and Buz woke up, crying about the Eedies. Kenny echoed their wailing and I took them all to our bed. This continued night after night. Byron said it was getting too crowded with all of us in a double bed. Something had to be done. "Find out what an Eedie is so we can get rid of it," he said. It was hard to get a description of an Eedie from a two-year-old and a three-year-old.

The following Saturday night, Byron and I went to Brunswick to see a movie, leaving reliable Betty in charge of the children for a few hours. Half way through the movie, a message flashed on the movie screen that read, "Mr. and Mrs. Worthen, please come to the office."

We got up and reported to the ticket office where they informed us that our babysitter had called and asked that we come home. The Eedies were there, and she couldn't handle it.

We rushed home in a panic, not knowing what we'd find when we got there. Betty opened the door when she heard us drive up. She looked exhausted. "I finally got them to sleep," she said. They had been crying about the Eedies. "What's an Eedie?" she asked. We told her we didn't know, but we'd destroy it when we found it.

The mystery was soon to be solved. On Monday, as the skies and the local forecaster promised rain, I hung my laundry upstairs. At 5:30 p.m., Byron arrived home from work; I happened to be in the living room with the children when he walked in. As he had done many times before, he strode dramatically across the room to the door that led to the upstairs rooms, closed it firmly, and said, "How many times do I have to tell you to keep that door closed? All the darn heat is going upstairs!" Patty and Buz huddled together, holding hands, their eyes wide with fright.

"I know what an Eedie is!" I announced. When Byron said, "All the darn heat is going upstairs," it sounded like "All the darn Eedies going upstairs!" As I often forgot to close that door, Byron often voiced his disapproval of the Eedies going upstairs.

That solved, I tried to remember to keep the door shut and Byron controlled his concern for the waste of heat. We explained to the children that Daddy wasn't mad at any Eedies, and life settled back to normal with Patty, Buz, and Kenny sleeping peacefully through the nights in their own beds.

Where the Eedies lived

14

The Man of Many Hats

THE NEAREST HOUSE to ours in Harpswell, Maine, was about one hundred yards away. Mr. Chase, a spry old gentleman, lived there and he held many important positions in the community. I believe these positions were self-appointed. The rest of the people who lived on the peninsula regarded him with tolerance and amusement but always with respect.

His daily job was that of a school bus driver. There was a one-room schoolhouse down the road that most of the children walked to. Mr. Chase owned a very old station wagon, and he picked up children at various houses and delivered them to the school. I observed his driving style, weaving all over the road. He wore very thick glasses and probably had cataracts. I asked some of the parents if they were concerned about Mr. Chase driving their children to school. They said, "Oh no. There's only one road between here and the school. We all avoid driving between 8 and 8:30 in the morning. He drives very slowly and the children arrive safely." The "school bus" waited at the school every day at 3:00 p.m. to pick up the children and drop them off at their houses. Mr. Chase wore a special cap and jacket to denote his status as a school bus driver.

We discovered he was also the fire chief. Shortly after we arrived in Harpswell, I asked Mrs. Palmer at the general store when the garbage truck would be coming to pick up the trash. She said there was no garbage service. She said we could either burn our garbage or deposit it at a designated dumping ground. We bought a special wire burn basket and set it on our driveway one day to burn our trash. As soon as Byron struck a match, Mr. Chase bolted out of his door and stood on his front porch, watching us. He went back in his house and came out with a fireman's hat and jacket on, got in his station wagon, and drove off. About five minutes later, he arrived in our driveway driving an antiquated fire truck. As he alighted, he shook his finger at us and said, "It's unlawful to burn anything!"

We explained we were being very careful and had the garden hose near us, but he insisted we put the fire out. When we complied, he climbed back in the fire truck and drove off. A few minutes later, he returned to his house in his station wagon.

That was not the end of Mr. Chase's official duties. One evening, Byron confided that there was going to be a readiness exercise at the air base. He said, "Some night soon, the phone will ring and I'll answer it and then I'll leave the house and drive to the base. Don't worry about anything, it's just a practice. And don't say anything to the neighbors if they ask you where I am. I might not be home for a couple of days."

Sure enough, about 2:00 a.m. one night the phone rang, Byron answered, said about two words, and then got dressed and drove off. I looked out of our bedroom window and saw lights going on in Mr. Chase's house, the general store, and even a house farther down the road. I realized then that we were all on a party line. When our phone rang, theirs did too. We all had a different type of ring to distinguish who the call was for, but they had no qualms about listening in to other people's conversations. It was part of their recreation. I suppose a phone ringing at 2:00 a.m. was too tempting to ignore.

At 7:00 a.m., I awoke to make breakfast for the children, and as I gazed out the sunporch windows, I saw a flurry of activity. There were many cars parked in front of the general store, and Mr. Chase was there wearing some sort of civil defense outfit, waving his arms, and shouting directions to people. I walked across the road and asked, "What's going on?" Bama (Mrs. Palmer), wringing her hands, said, "You just never know! You just never know!" Mr. Chase was telling one man to drive into town and buy cases of bottled water and bandages. The rest of them were directed to go inside the general store for a civil defense meeting.

I wanted to tell these panic-stricken people that it was just a practice and didn't concern them, but I couldn't. Mr. Chase was designating the basement under the general store as the official air raid shelter.

It was several days before Byron came home and everyone calmed down. The neighborhood returned to its normal peaceful mode of living. Every now and then, I watch that old comedic movie, *The Russians are Coming*, and it reminds me of that time and those dear people.

15

The Heart and Soul of Harpswell

THE PRIMARY OCCUPATION in this community is lobster fishing. Outside of almost every house, you could see a pile of wooden lobster crates. For some, it was a full-time occupation, and for others, it was done part-time, supplementing a primary job in the town of Brunswick. Farming was also done, but not on a great scale as the land between the ocean waters was narrow and sometimes rocky.

The day after we moved into our house, I answered a knock at the back door. There stood a man in overalls and rubber boots holding a bucket. He said, "Hi, I'm Ernest Moody. I live over there in back of the general store. Welcome to the neighborhood. I brought you a little something." He lifted the bucket and handed it to me.

I smiled and thanked him, reaching for the handle of the bucket. When I looked down and saw what was in it, I screamed and dropped it. Ernest looked perplexed. I said, "Take it away!" It was a horrible dark-green giant bug with antennae and groping claws. "What is it?" I asked. "It's just a lobster, caught this morning. Thought you might like it for your supper tonight."

Being from the midwest, far from seafood, I had never seen a lobster before. "Thank you very much, but we don't eat lobster," I said. That evening, I told Byron about the experience. He said, "What? You refused it? Are you crazy?" I told him I didn't even know what a lobster was, much less how to cook it. "You just put it in a big pot of boiling water. It's delicious!"

"You mean you cook it while it's alive? Looking at you with those beady black eyes?" He nodded, and I told him I could never do that, even if it was the ugliest creature I had ever seen.

Ernest Moody was Irene's husband. Irene was one of Mr. and Mrs. Palmer's daughters. I met Irene the following day, and as mentioned earlier, we became lifelong friends. Irene makes the best lobster stew you ever tasted. Of course, it's loaded with butter and cream.

Irene had two younger sisters who babysat for us on occasion. Betty was still in high school, and Ann was nineteen and helped her parents in the store. She was an exceptionally beautiful girl. Unfortunately, she had developed a gum disease several years previously and had to have all her teeth pulled. She wore dentures, which nobody could detect because they looked so natural.

Ann would delight our children by taking her teeth out and performing all kinds of tricks with them. Every time she came over, Patty and Buz begged, "Take your teeth out, Ann."

Ann had many boyfriends, and she took her teeth out to amuse them too. Apparently, it was not a turnoff because she didn't lack for dates.

One Saturday afternoon, when I stepped into the general store, a fragrance permeated the whole store. "What is that smell?" I asked. It seemed to be coming from the door that led to their kitchen and living quarters. "Oh, that's the baked beans," Mrs. Palmer answered. I found out that everyone on the peninsula made their own baked beans from scratch every Saturday. Friday night, the hard dried beans were put in water to soak.

Early the next morning, they were put into a crock with a combination of ingredients and were slow-cooked in the oven all day to be consumed on Saturday night. The Palmers invited us to come over for supper that evening. Who could resist that tempting aroma?

At supper that evening, I became aware that I had never known the taste of real homemade baked beans. I had always thought of beans as something in a can that you used as an accompaniment to hot dogs. Mrs.

Palmer gave me the recipe, and I started making my own baked beans, starting with the little round hard dried pea beans.

Apparently, a few of those dried beans fell on the floor one Saturday while I was cooking. Little Buz, then two years old, tugged on my apron and pointed to his nose. I tipped his head back and saw a dried bean buried way back in his nostril. I tried to extricate it but was afraid I would poke it farther back, so I called Irene to ask where the nearest doctor was in the area. She said there were no doctors but she knew a nurse, and she climbed into our car to show us the way to her house.

The nurse put Buz on her kitchen table and got out some tweezers. While talking to him very calmly, she carefully probed and captured the bean. Everyone smiled with relief, and Buz was congratulated for being a brave boy. We arrived home and I went back to my cooking when I felt a tug at my apron. Looking down, I saw Buz pointing at his nose and another bean that was stuck! We had to repeat the whole process, but first I swept the kitchen floor and made sure there were no more beans for him to find.

Another visitor knocked on our back door a few days after we moved in. He introduced himself as the pastor of the church down the road. There was only one church in the community, a Baptist church, and everyone went to it every Sunday. Obviously, he didn't rely totally on the offering for his livelihood because he told me if we needed any fields to be plowed or other farmwork, he could do that type of work. Apparently, the surrounding land belonged to the house, but we had no plans to farm it.

The church was one of the places people congregated, not only to worship, but for fellowship, conversation, passing along news tidbits about neighbors. Remember, there was no television during those days and very little opportunity for recreation. The other place people flocked to was the one-room schoolhouse once a month for the parent-teacher meeting. Everyone went to that whether they had children in school or not. It was a social evening, a chance to share stories and enjoy cakes and cookies.

The Christmas season arrived and the pastor, dressed in a Santa Claus suit, opened the church one Saturday afternoon so the children could have the opportunity of telling Santa what they wanted for Christmas.

Sitting on a chair at the altar, he lifted each child onto his lap and listened patiently to their wishes. There was a long line in the aisle leading to the altar, but it was our turn at last. Buz was the first to climb onto Santa's lap. This was his very first encounter with Santa. The pastor smiled, patted his head, and said, "Well, little boy, and what do you want?" Buz was thoughtful for a few seconds while he looked around the church, and then, looking the pastor straight in the eyes, he said, "Ohhh, I'll have a beer!"

I was so embarrassed. And in a church! Buz slipped off the pastor's knees and ran cheerfully back to me while Patty was lifted onto Santa's lap. A perfect little lady, she straightened her skirt and recited a long list of her desires.

One Saturday night, we were invited to Mr. and Mrs. Palmer's living quarters after store hours. There we discovered another delightful tradition. Every Saturday night, Mrs. Palmer made dozens and dozens of doughnuts. Their kitchen was extremely large. Mrs. Palmer stood at a big black old-fashioned woodstove, dropping doughnuts into a vat of hot grease and retrieving them at the precise proper time to drain on absorbent paper, then transferring them to a platter. From that point, the doughnuts were sprinkled with confectioners' sugar or cinnamon and sugar. Sometimes, they were left just plain, which was my favorite.

A large blue enamelware coffeepot was on the stove, and everyone helped themselves to the coffee. The doughnut platters were placed on the huge round oilcloth-covered kitchen table, and everyone sat around talking, eating doughnuts, telling jokes, and just enjoying each other's company. Some of the neighbors drifted in to partake of the delicious doughnuts and to join in the conversation.

That evening, I realized we had become accepted into these people's lives. Irene confided some time later that everyone had been afraid we would be "city people," aloof and uninterested in their simple lives. We were honored to be included in their warm friendship. We formed bonds as close as any kinship could be.

While Mrs. Palmer, whom I will refer to as Bama from now on, was busily making doughnuts, I started telling the family about my first date with Byron, my train trip to California, and Patty's first oil bath. Bama laughed so hard she had to sit down and tears rolled down her flushed cheeks. Her daughters had to take over the doughnut-making. From then on, we had a standing invitation to the Saturday night social hour at Bama and Bampa's house.

Eventually, Mr. Chase, the man of many hats, conceded that we weren't city folks after all. One day, he walked over to our house and asked if I would, by any chance, happen to have some paregoric. He had a stomachache, and he didn't have any more of this home remedy. Luckily, I had a bottle that Byron's grandfather had given me. Grandpa Van Brocklin had a basement full of herbs and home remedies. He told me to put a few drops of paregoric in the baby's bottle to make him sleep. I never used it and never intended to use it, so I gave Mr. Chase the whole bottle and told him he could keep it.

Mr. Chase looked at me with a new respect after that. Being in possession of paregoric redeemed my mistake of burning garbage in the driveway. Years later, I discovered that paregoric was an alcoholic mixture of opium and camphor. Imagine, people had been putting this in their babies' bottles!

16

Lonely Nights

IN AUGUST 1952, Byron received orders to go to Korea. We said good-bye to our dear Harpswell friends and the children and I moved back to our house on 34 George Street, Manchester, New Hampshire.

Byron was stationed in Seoul, Korea, for a year. The war between North and South Korea was in full force. I wrote long letters every day telling Byron what the children had been doing, what they were learning, and how much I missed him. Every day, I waited eagerly for the mailman to bring a letter from Byron, assuring me that he was all right. Sometimes several days went by with no letters. Then three or four letters came at once. It took about a week for his letters to reach me.

Personal computers hadn't been invented yet, so there was no e-mail or Skype. Cell phones would not be invented for fifty more years. Each day, I prayed that he would be safe. Each day, Byron missed his little family.

Patty started kindergarten in September. Buz and Kenny played with the neighborhood children. They were happy, active children, learning new things every day. I was learning from them as I watched their individual personalities develop. Our days were busy and passed quickly. In the evenings, after their supper, baths, and bedtime stories, I would read parts of Byron's letters to them. They enjoyed this as there was usually a little note for each of them in each letter.

During that year, television sets were becoming available for sale. Until that time, most people watched TV by looking in the window of electronic stores. There were large crowds in front of those stores when football games were being televised.

I bought our first TV in October 1952. It was an Emerson black-and-white. There was no color TV at that time. There were three channels to watch, and all channels turned off at midnight. The *Today Show* with Dave Garroway entered our home bringing us news, weather, and a glimpse of the true personalities of the hosts of this unrehearsed live show. We were accustomed to watching movies that had been carefully directed, rehearsed, and edited. Live television was a novelty. Watching someone burst into laughter after making a mistake was refreshing and endearing. We felt close to them and welcomed them into our homes as family.

Byron's brother and family lived in the downstairs apartment. After our children were asleep, my sister-in-law came upstairs and we watched *I Love Lucy*. Jackie Gleason in *The Honeymooners* was also a favorite. The children watched *Howdy Doody* in the morning. That was about the extent of our television entertainment in 1952.

A new card game, *canasta*, became popular in the early 1950s. When we weren't watching *Lucy* or some other comedy show, my sister-in-law and I were engrossed in challenging games of *canasta*.

The year passed. The children grew. We welcomed Byron home in the summer of 1953, and the lonely nights became a memory. Orders arrived and we started packing to move to Newburgh, New York.

17

Ruby
The Inspector General of Circle Lane

PRECISELY AT EIGHT fifteen in the morning, while the last school-age child in the neighborhood runs for the school bus, Ruby steps out of her front door and the housewives of Circle Lane spring into action. The challenge has begun!

We are living in Kroll's Acres, a housing development in Gardnertown, New York, near Newburgh. Byron completed his year in Korea and is stationed at Stewart Air Force Base. Our house is on a cul-de-sac. Most of the neighbors are Air Force personnel and their families. The wives are all in their mid-twenties and the children all range from newborn to six years of age.

In 1953, none of the wives worked. Each household had one car. If the wife needed the car for shopping or errands, it was easy for the husband to get a ride to the air force base from one of the neighbors.

On 68 Circle Lane, we were sandwiched between two war brides. On one side lived an air force lieutenant and his beautiful German wife, Elena. Elena met her husband when the war was over and United States military personnel occupied Germany to help restore and rebuild the country. Elena took English lessons in Germany so she could speak with her husband's family when she came to the United States. Unfortunately, his parents were French-Canadians who lived in Maine and didn't speak English.

Ivy was from England. She lived in the house on the other side of us. Her first husband was in the Royal Air Force and was killed during the war, leaving her with a son. After the war, she met Randy, an air force sergeant. They married and Randy adopted the boy.

There was a great deal of neighborly spirit on Circle Lane. When one of the wives was pregnant, the others got together and gave her a baby shower. There were a lot of baby showers going on during our time in Kroll's Acres, including one for me as our Barbara was born in 1956.

We swapped children's clothes, books, recipes, and babysitting favors. When one of us was in the hospital having a baby, all the others pitched in and watched her other children, making sure the family had a good supper each night. The camaraderie among the wives on Circle Lane was unsurpassed by any women's group I had ever known. This was probably the result of one person: *Ruby*.

Ruby lived at the end of the cul-de-sac. She and her husband had no children, but she was an expert on how children should be raised. Her floors were cleaned, waxed, and polished to a blinding shine. Not one cookie crumb or sneaker skid mark marred their pristine state. By 8:00 a.m., her laundry hung on the line in a precise arrangement. Her sheets, towels, and husband's T-shirts were the whitest on the street. Her flower garden adorned the front and side of her house with healthy brilliant flowers and not a weed dared to reside there.

In other words, Ruby was perfect. She set a standard that none of us could reach. Faced with getting our children fed and ready for school, loads of soiled diapers (there were no disposable diapers) and babies demanding our attention, there was no way we could measure up to Ruby's standards. But we were all determined to try. And that determination formed the basis of a sisterhood as loyal as any sorority.

Ruby stands on her front stoop and surveys her territory. She will stop at four houses on the left side of the street, spending fifteen minutes at each house. Then she will cross the street and do the same thing with those four houses as she heads toward her home. This will bring her home in two hours, having gathered and spread neighborhood news at each house. She will be home in time to bring in her laundry, fold it, put it away, and wipe up any paw marks her Siamese cat may have made on her floors from the litter box dust.

My house is the third one in line. I have thirty minutes to achieve perfection. The race is on! At 8:45, my phone rings. Elena says, "She just left. She's headed for your house."

I run a critical scrutiny of my domain. Breakfast dishes are washed, dried, and put away.

Sink is scrubbed and gleaming. Counters are spotless. Floor is swept. Laundry is swishing in the wringer-washer in the basement. Three-year-old Kenny is happily playing with toys in the living room. Fresh coffee is perking on the stove. Table is set with a clean white tablecloth, two cups and saucers, spoons, napkins. A small plate of cookies graces the center of the table. A knock at the back door!

On my way to the door, I quickly check the kitchen chairs for any globs of jelly, syrup, or (heaven forbid) bubble gum. In walks Ruby. Ruby walks through the kitchen and sticks her head in the living room to wave to Kenny and returns to sit at the table while I pour the coffee. Ruby always takes just one cookie. Her first words will be about her visit at the previous house.

"I just left Elena's and that poor girl has so much wax buildup on her kitchen floor! She's going to have to get down and really scrub to get rid of it. You know, you have to be careful when you wax at the edges and corners. She's going to have to use some strong stuff to get that down to the bare linoleum."

The rest of the conversation is about her cat and his latest antics. I must admit he is a most extraordinary cat, and I enjoy hearing about his adventures. Next, the discussion turns to how her garden is doing. Her portulaca and salvia are brilliant. Ruby never spread mean gossip about any of us. Three minutes are left. Ruby asks how my children are and walks toward the door. After a brief farewell, the door closes and I reach for the phone. "Ivy? She's on her way." Ivy says, "Thanks" and slams the phone down.

Fifteen minutes later as I am hanging clothes on the line, I see Ruby cross the street to Joyce's house. I finish hanging the laundry and go inside to call Ivy. "Ivy? Did I pass?"

"No. When she looked in the living room, she saw one of your kid's socks sticking out from under an armchair. Also, there was dust on your TV."

We didn't take Ruby's criticisms to heart. We didn't have a rivalry between us to be the best. It was a game. We knew we couldn't meet Ruby's expectations. We just wanted to make it harder for her to find something wrong. In the process, we all got our work done quickly and thoroughly and found we had time to gather in the afternoons and relax on one of our front lawns while all of our children played together.

For Ruby, the neighborhood visits were her only raison d'être. If she had been born in a later era, she probably would have had a successful career. But this was 1953. Men had careers. Women raised the next generation.

We all knew we had something very special that Ruby didn't have. Despite the peanut butter fingerprints on the refrigerator, the crayons and papers scattered throughout the house, and the dirty socks under the armchairs, we had something precious. We had the scent of young children, fresh from their evening bath, damp hair so kissable. We had giggling, wriggling kids romping on our bed, wrestling and hugging and kissing us before they settled down for bedtime. We had the best! We all knew it. Byron and I knew it as the house quieted down for the night, and we knew we were the luckiest people in the world.

18

Monster Bread

WE WERE ALL looking forward to my father's visit. The children loved to listen to his stories, spoken in his soft musical Swedish accent. My dear mother had passed away recently, and I knew how much my father missed her.

In honor of his visit, I decided to bake something that Mom often made—Swedish coffee bread. Baking with yeast always intimidated me so I avoided it. I put my fears aside and rummaged through my recipe box until I found the recipe my friend in New Hampshire had given me.

The day before Dad arrived, I assembled the ingredients and followed the recipe carefully. Setting the dough aside to let rise, I went to work cleaning the house, putting a small vase of fresh flowers in the guest room, and getting rid of clutter. When I returned to the kitchen, I was relieved to see that the dough had risen successfully and all I had to do was bake it.

The directions were "Divide the dough in thirds, braid, and let rise again." I divided the dough into three equal parts, rolled each part into a long strip, and started to braid the three strips together. It was beginning to look much larger than I thought it should, but I continued braiding. I had to put the finished product on a cookie sheet because it wouldn't fit in a bread pan. Then I set it aside to rise one more time.

An hour later, I checked on it, and it was beginning to resemble a small bed pillow. I figured I had let it rise too long, so into the oven it went. I cleaned up the flour mess in the kitchen, happy that I was making something special for my father.

Thirty minutes later, the kitchen had that delicious "baking bread" aroma I could even smell the distinctive cardamom spice that makes Swedish coffee bread so good. It must be almost ready to take out. I opened the oven door and was horrified to see that the "bed pillow" had grown and was filling up my oven. It took another hour to form a crust and I finally took it out.

Byron came home from work and saw the monster bread cooling on the kitchen table. "What's that?" he asked. "It's Swedish coffee bread like my mother used to make," I answered with a defensive attitude that dared him to comment on its size. Byron was a smart man. He said, "Smells good," as he walked past it.

When the bread had cooled, I cut a small piece and tasted it. It tasted good, just the right amount of cardamom flavor. But I couldn't let Dad see what it looked like. What could I wrap it in? The only thing I could wrap it in was a garbage bag. Where can I hide it? Not on the counter. It would take up too much room. The only place large enough was the cupboard under the kitchen sink. That was its home for the next few days.

Dad rode the train from Chicago to Newburgh, New York. We met him at the train station the next day, and when he was settled in the living room with the children snuggling with him, I asked him if he'd like some coffee and coffee bread. He brightened up and said, "Ya, sure," and started to get up. I panicked and told him to stay right there, I would bring it to him.

I took the bread out of its hiding place, cut a huge slice, then sliced that piece into six pieces, put them on a serving plate, and brought it to the living room. He enjoyed it and said it was just like Mom's coffee bread.

For the next few days, I kept the bread under the sink and took it out to slice when Dad was occupied in another part of the house. There were a few times I heard his footsteps approaching the kitchen while I was slicing, and I furtively stuffed the bread in the garbage bag and threw it under the sink.

After we saw Dad off at the train station, I called my friend in New Hampshire and asked her why the bread turned out so huge. She said, "The recipe makes three loaves. The directions were 'divide in three and braid,' but you should have divided each of those three sections into three again, and then braided."

It didn't matter. I never made Swedish coffee bread again.

19

Buz Is Disowned

OUR TWO OLDEST children were now in school at Gardnertown Elementary. Patty was in second grade. Buz was in first grade. In 1954, children didn't wear jeans to school. Girls wore dresses and boys wore shirts and trousers. After school, they changed into play clothes and played outside until the *Mickey Mouse Club* was on TV at 5:00 p.m.

One day, when Buz arrived home from school, his good clothes and shoes were covered with mud. I wondered why the teachers would let the kids play in a muddy area during recess. The next day, after sending him to school with clean clothes and shoes, he came home in the same muddy condition. *Hmmm, the teachers aren't watching these kids very well during recess*, I thought. I might have to look into this.

The following morning, I sent him off in a clean outfit and warned him to stay away from the mud on the playground. About five minutes later, as I was cleaning the kitchen counter, I discovered that Buz had forgotten to take his lunch box. I drove to the school and arrived just as his bus was unloading its passengers.

A teacher, Miss Kurtz, was herding the children off the bus and into the school. I got out of the car with the lunch box and arrived at the curb just as Buz was stepping out of the bus. Miss Kurtz grabbed Buz before his feet left the last step of the bus. Shaking her finger in Buz's face, she screamed, "Didn't I tell you never to come to school like this again?"

I looked at Buz. He was covered with mud. His shoes, trousers, and shirt had globs of gray mud dripping off them. Miss Kurtz, furious and still holding on to Buz, turned her head and saw me. "Look at this kid! This is the way he comes to school every day. I'd like to know what kind of mother would send her kid to school looking like this. Do you know her?"

Buz and I exchanged a quick glance. I shrugged my shoulders and backed away from the ranting Miss Kurtz, shaking my head no, and got back in my car with the lunch box.

That afternoon, I met Buz at the bus stop. "Okay, Buz. Where did you get into the mud?" He showed me an area not far from the bus stop where there was deep oozing mud. It was just the consistency that a six-year-old would revel in, stomping around while waiting for the school bus.

He was instructed never to step in that puddle again, and as far as I know, he never did.

In 1954, teachers had complete control of their students. While the children were in school, teachers were the surrogate parents and exercised the right to discipline by any method they deemed effective. Unfortunately, there were a few teachers like Miss Kurtz who misused their authority. I learned more about her much later from Buz.

20

Green Gravy

MY MOTHER WAS an excellent cook. Not only did everything she made taste good, but her presentation made your mouth water. Even the table scraps for the dog were attractively arranged in his bowl. Her baked goods were the envy of all the wives in the neighborhood.

Sadly, she did not pass her skills on to her children. Mom preferred to prepare her meals by herself with no help or interference from anyone. The only help she expected was for drying the dishes after the evening meal.

My sister had the foresight to go to cooking classes during the months before her wedding. It never entered my head to do the same before my marriage. The only formal domestic instructions I received were in school. In the seventh grade, I learned how to make a pot of cocoa.

One day, when I was about seventeen, I visited my sister who was married and living in Chicago. I asked her if I could help her with anything while she made dinner. She handed me a bunch of spinach and told me to wash it. I filled the sink with hot water and soap and put the spinach in. It quickly turned to a soapy mush before my sister turned around to check my progress.

But the worst cooking faux pas happened after I had been married for over six years and had quite a few good meals to my credit. We were living in Newburgh, New York, and my brother-in-law (Mildred's husband, Bill) was planning to drive east on business. Since he would be in our vicinity at Thanksgiving, I invited him to our house for Thanksgiving dinner.

Wanting to impress him, I looked through several magazines for new ideas to cook a turkey. I found one that sounded good. Soak a dish towel in melted butter and spread it over the turkey before putting it in the oven. It was supposed to keep the turkey moist and tender.

Well, that made sense to me. I decided to buy a new dish towel for the occasion rather than use one of my old ones. I found a nice bright green-and-white checked towel and followed the instructions, carefully placing it over the turkey after soaking it in butter.

About three hours later, I lifted the towel to see how the turkey looked, and to my surprise, the whole breast was green-and-white checked. Not only that, but the juice at the bottom of the pan was bright green!

What a dilemma! The potatoes were ready to mash, and everything else was nearing completion. *Well, maybe it won't look so green after I add the flour and water*, I thought. Wrong! It was the prettiest spring-green gravy you ever saw. "Maybe it won't look so green when it's poured on the mashed potatoes." So while everyone was busy passing bowls and helping themselves to turkey, I went around the table holding the gravy bowl high in the air and offering to put the gravy on everyone's potatoes. When I came to Bill, he said, "No, I'll put the gravy on by myself." I insisted, so he sat back while I daintily drizzled a sparse amount of gravy on his potatoes, hoping he wouldn't notice the color. His immediate response was "Why is the gravy green?" I just said, "It's a new recipe," and passed the gravy bowl on to the next person. No further questions were asked.

21

A Pain in the Neck

FEBRUARY 26, 1956, was a cold, snowy night. I was expecting our fourth child. As we were watching television, I started having contractions. They soon were coming at three-minute intervals, but they weren't like the contractions I had experienced with the previous babies.

"I'm not sure these are labor contractions," I told Byron. He suggested I call the nurse's desk at the West Point Army Hospital and describe them. The nurse asked, "This is your fourth baby?" I said, "Yes, but the contractions don't start at my back and come around toward the front." The nurse said, "I don't care if the contractions are in your big toe. If they're three minutes apart, get yourself here NOW!"

We drove over the mountain road in a blinding snowstorm. I was herded to the labor room, and Byron was allowed to remain in the room with me. This was the first time he had been with me during childbirth.

The doctor came in and examined me. He said, "Oh, it will be another hour or so." He left the room. During the next contraction, I felt I was going to burst. My eyes were closed, but I was seeing pinwheels and sky rockets on the closed lids as I struggled to push the baby into the world. Then I heard Byron. He was sitting in a chair next to my bed. His head was on my bed facedown. His head was very close to my face. "Alice," he was saying, "I have a pain in the back of my neck. Could you rub it for me?" I opened my eyes and noticed my hand was within inches from his head, and it was closed in a fist. How tempting! Between clenched teeth, I replied, "I can't. I'm busy now."

During the next contraction, I heard a strange sound. It sounded like a cow mooing. Then I realized it was me. "The baby's here," I informed Byron. "Oh no," he said. "The doctor said it will be another hour."

"Well, then there's a basketball down there. Lift up the sheet." Byron obeyed and scrambled out the door looking for the doctor.

The doctor was running in the hall toward my room. "The baby's here," Byron yelled.

"I know! I heard that sound like a cow mooing and I know what that means." They both jostled each other, trying to get through the door at the same time. Barbara Sue Worthen had already presented herself.

22

A Storybook House

BYRON CAME HOME from work one day in June 1957 and said, "Get the kids together. I'm taking you all for a ride."

"Where?"

"It's a surprise. You'll see."

Out on country roads, we rode, farther and farther away from Gardnertown. My curiosity had peaked. "Byron, where are we going?"

"You'll see."

The children started guessing games, but Byron just smiled. We came to a large pond and Byron turned onto a narrow road. A short ride later, we turned onto Station Road. We crossed a small bridge that spanned a stream and stopped at a house. White porticoes framed the front entrance. There was a circular driveway, a tennis court, and a storybook wishing well. A large tree reached out one of its limbs that supported an old-fashioned swing. Perennial flowers bloomed around the house, and there were rose bushes in bloom.

"Who lives here?" I asked. "We do, if you like it." Byron produced a key. "Come on. Take a look."

"You want to move? Nobody in the Air Force moves while they are still at their duty station. We've been here three years. You could get orders to move away any time."

The children were anxious to get out and explore. "Well, come inside and look around. I heard about this place and I came out here on my lunch hour."

Byron unlocked the front door and we entered a spacious front hall. Facing us was the stairway leading upstairs. On our right was a doorway leading to a beautiful dining room.

It was furnished with a dark cherry dining table and chairs, an elegant china cabinet, and a sideboard.

On our left, we stepped into a living room that measured the length of the house. There was a real fireplace at the far end. Two comfortable-looking lounge chairs were next to the fireplace. Between two windows stood an old-fashioned secretary writing desk that had glass doors above and a drop-down panel that opened to reveal quaint cubbyholes and tiny drawers. There was even a place for an inkwell. Inkwells had become a relic of the past by 1957 as ballpoint pens had become the writing tool of choice.

Our living room furniture would easily fit in here with room to spare. We walked the length of the room and arrived at the red brick fireplace. I envisioned the children hanging stockings on Christmas Eve. Turning right, we entered a hall that had storage rooms on each side. The hall led to the kitchen.

It was a typical country kitchen with plenty of room. I pictured our kitchen table by the set of windows where the sun was streaming in. At one wall stood a sturdy white cabinet like my mother had when I was a little girl. It had a metal counter that pulled out to make room to roll pie crusts. It even had a special door that housed a large flour sifter. The cupboards above were roomy. Something caught my eye. There, on the wall, was a coffee grinder with a hand crank. This kitchen was definitely reminiscent of the 1920s.

My mind raced around. Imagine! Eating breakfast in this big cheerful kitchen. Having dinner every night in a beautiful formal dining room.

We didn't own dining room furniture, but there it was, already furnished. There were even tablecloths in the sideboard.

"Byron, how much is the rent?"
"Same as we're paying now."

The children had been playing on the swing and exploring the outdoors. Now they came in and clambered up the stairs. Squeals of delight echoed in the empty rooms. "Wow! I've got dibs on *this* room." Well, I had to see what was so great. At the top of the stairs, I could see there were four bedrooms and a bathroom. Each bedroom was big and had many windows. I chose our bedroom immediately. It looked out on the driveway, wishing well, swing, and tennis court.

"I'll have my very own bedroom now!" exclaimed Patty. Our present house had only two small downstairs bedrooms. Barbara's crib was in Patty's room. Byron and I were in the other bedroom. The boys shared a small attic room that was adequate, but unfinished and had a small attic window.

I looked out the windows of the beautiful room the boys had staked out. Adjoining the spacious grounds was a field of young sweet corn about eighteen inches tall. The stream we had passed was catching the late summer sun in its ripples. A young girl was riding a horse. Wildflowers graced the sides of the road. I was already planning where our furniture would be placed.

It was an ideal place for the children. The boys picked strawberries for the farmer down the road and were paid ten cents for each pint. That was a fortune for a seven-year-old and a nine-year-old.

On hot days, I packed a lunch and the children and I walked to the pond. I sat on the bank with Barbara while the children went wading. Our German shepherd enjoyed swimming with the children, but kept a watchful eye on Kenny and nudged him back toward the shore if he thought the boy was getting too near the deep water.

When the sweet corn was ready to pick, the farmer told me to help myself. What a delight it was to put a pot of water on the stove to boil while I stepped outside and picked the corn for supper.

In the fall and spring, when the boys got home from school, they took their fishing rods down to the creek and spent hours fishing and hunting for turtles and frogs. They brought the fish home for me to cook. Ken kept a frog under his cap. I didn't know that until I asked him to remove his cap at the dinner table one night.

Patty had a friend down the road who was her age. She had another friend who let her ride her horse. For an eleven-year-old girl, that was a dream come true. The woods in back of our house were fun for the whole family to explore. Byron took the boys with him to hunt pheasants, but came home empty-handed.

That year, a fire crackling in the brick fireplace made our Christmas Eve a memorable one. But the big surprise on Christmas morning was when we came downstairs and saw Santa's sooty footprints on the hearth. Ken was very impressed and remembers it to this day.

Barbara was my constant companion that year, toddling around the backyard while I hung up the washed clothes, helping me pick wildflowers, and playing in the big kitchen while I ironed or prepared meals.

The year passed quickly. The farmer's corn was once more standing in straight rows, about twelve inches high. We were all eagerly looking forward to another summer on Station Road.

On June 7, 1958, Byron came home with orders to go to Japan.

Story Book House, 1957

Red Brick Fireplace

23

Good Morning, Japan

CHIYO-SAN CAME TO our house a few days after we arrived in Japan. The employment office at the air base sent her to us. She remained with us for the four years we were there.

Hired to be a housemaid for our family, she became a gentle matriarch, loving friend, guardian, and beloved grandmother to all of us.

Early one morning, there was a knock at my door. I opened it, and there stood a short, slim woman in her mid-fifties with a tan weathered face. She bowed and said, "*Ohayo*," which meant "Good morning" as I found out much later. It is pronounced like Ohio, so I thought she was asking if we came from Ohio. So I said, "No, New York." She looked puzzled as she came into the house.

Not knowing she didn't understand English, I elaborated on our original birthplaces. "Well, I'm originally from Illinois and my husband was born in New Hampshire, but we were living in New York before we came here."

I was getting no response, so I spread a map of the United States on the table and pointed out Ohio and New York. She opened her *furoshiki* (a large square cloth tied together on all four corners), put on an apron, and started washing the breakfast dishes. All day she worked quietly around the house, sweeping, dusting, doing the laundry. Occasionally, she would hum a song. At five o'clock, she took her apron off, said "*Sayonara*," and left.

The next morning, she appeared at the door, bowed, and said, "New York." She thought I had taught her how to say "Good Morning" in English.

Chiyo with Barbara

24

Blackie's Downfall

OUR FAMILY HAD barely settled into our new surroundings in Japan when Patty, Buz, and Kenny explored the small town just outside the gates of the base.

Each of them came home proudly carrying a small plastic bag containing a goldfish swimming around in a small amount of water.

I wasn't particularly happy about the new pets, but I went to town to buy a fishbowl, some fish food, and a small net. I told the children they would be responsible for feeding the fish and cleaning the bowl when needed.

In a few days, the fishbowl needed cleaning, and I gathered the children into the bathroom to demonstrate the proper way to clean a fishbowl. With the fishnet in one hand and the bowl in the other, I put on my "teaching voice" and said, "Now pay attention because you are going to be doing this. First, you empty the dirty water from the fishbowl." With that, I inverted the fishbowl over the toilet and dumped the contents, including the fish.

I knew immediately that I had forgotten a step; first, take the fish out of the bowl. Patty, Buz, and Kenny watched in horror as their fish swam around the toilet. "Don't worry," I reassured them. I'll get them out of there."

Using the fishnet, I tried to retrieve the fish, but they darted away from the net the minute it touched the water. Two of the fish retreated to a small hole and disappeared forever. The only fish remaining was the black fish that belonged to Kenny.

Kenny was visibly distressed. "Mom, you have to save Blackie. Don't let him go in that hole." Calmly, I assured him that I would rescue Blackie. After waiting about ten minutes to allow Blackie and me to calm down, I gingerly lowered the net by Blackie's tail. The second the net touched the water, Blackie headed for that hole. Kenny gasped and I withdrew the net. Both of us peered into the hole for signs of life. Slowly, we saw Blackie's head peek out from the safety of the hole. "He's still there!" Kenny exclaimed.

Minutes turned into hours as Blackie and I played the game of hide-and-seek. Eventually, people needed to use the toilet, and this was the only bathroom in the house. I sent the children to the neighbor's to use their facilities.

Five o'clock came and Byron arrived home from work to find me on my knees guarding the toilet. "Don't use the toilet!" I warned him.

"Why not?"

"Because Blackie's in there." A look of defiance flashed in his eyes until he saw Kenny's anxious face. Then he offered suggestions, which we tried with no success.

We had a silent supper. Kenny couldn't eat much. Darkness came and I made a great discovery. When I went into the dark bathroom and turned on the light, there was Blackie happily swimming around the toilet bowl. He quickly dashed into the hole when he realized there was light in the room. I had a solution! I turned off the light and armed myself with our flashlight. Hiding behind the bathroom door, I waited several minutes to give Blackie a feeling of freedom, then armed with the flashlight and net, I quickly aimed the flashlight at the toilet, switched it on, and frantically tried to catch Blackie in the net.

Blackie was too quick for me. I actually think he was enjoying this game. Byron offered to man the flashlight to give me more time and accuracy with the net. Each time, we got closer to catching Blackie, but he eluded us. Kenny kept watch over the rescue efforts until it was way past bedtime for a seven-year-old.

"Kenny, you have to go to bed."

"No, you're going to flush Blackie away!"

"No, I'm not. We're going to get him out of there."

"You promise you won't flush him?"

"Kenny, I promise you I will not flush Blackie!"

Reluctantly, he went to his bedroom. I tucked him in and promised, again, that Blackie would be in his fishbowl by morning. By eleven o'clock, Byron announced he had had enough of this, and he had to use the toilet. I blocked the bathroom door and reminded him that we promised Kenny. I suggested he use the neighbor's bathroom.

Byron said, "I have some serious business with that toilet and I am not going to a neighbor that I haven't even met to ask to use their toilet at eleven o'clock at night!"

I saw the futility of any further effort, so I gave up. Byron was kind enough to flush Blackie away before he put the toilet to further use, and I turned my thoughts to what I was going to say to Kenny in the morning. He was going to lose trust in his mother. It could affect him for life.

By morning, I had my story ready. Kenny woke up early and ran to the bathroom to find Blackie. I followed him in, put my arms around him, and told him Blackie had gone. "You flushed him!"

"No, I didn't." Well, that was the truth. I said, "Blackie really wanted to join his brother and sister so he finally left. By now, he is probably in some big lake, happily swimming around, not confined to a small fishbowl."

And so, Kenny and I will always remember Blackie, and we hope he found his brother and sister.

25

Japan
First Year

D URING OUR FIRST year in Japan, I kept busy with social
events on the air force base. There were various groups that
I joined: the bowling league, the officers' wives club, etc. The officers'
wives club planned to put on a show featuring music and dancing from
the early 1900s through the 1940s. I joined the rehearsals for that show,
and we worked on it constantly for three months. It turned out to be a
hit, and we were asked for repeat performances. The noncommissioned
officer's club heard about it and asked us to perform at their club also.

Can-can girls. Alice is second from left

Jitterbug. Alice is the sailor

Stage door canteen scene, wives club show

In the spring of 1959, I formed a group of ladies who were interested in learning Japanese flower arranging and found a dear teacher who came to our house once a week. She dressed in traditional *kimono* and *zori* (footwear).

She did not speak one word of English, but we were able to learn a few Japanese words from her. The flowers were named Father, Mother, Visitor, and Children. The tallest flower was the father and it stood straight. The mother was about three-fourths the height of the father and leaned back at an angle so she was looking up to the father. The visitor was in a place of prominence on the other side, and the children were of varying heights in the middle.

I also asked around to see if there was a dancing teacher who would teach Barbara Japanese dancing. The older children were in school, and there weren't many small children in our neighborhood for Barbara to play with so I thought this might be interesting for her.

I opened the door one afternoon and met the prettiest Japanese lady I had ever seen. Her name was Yoshiko. I called Barbara into the living room, and Yoshiko spoke to her in a soft musical voice. I found that Yoshiko didn't speak English either. She put a record on the turntable and started to dance a simple folk dance, encouraging Barbara to join her.

Barbara watched with admiration, but was too shy to try it herself. The dance looked like fun, and I joined the dance teacher, hoping Barbara would give it a try. It was not an activity that interested a three-year-old, but I found it exhilarating. By the end of the session, Barbara had resumed playing with dolls in her bedroom, and I asked the teacher if she would teach me.

Little did I know that I was on the way to becoming a Japanese dance teacher and would be performing on television four years later in the United States. But that's another story.

Yoshiko

The summer was fast approaching. The children would soon be out of school. I was elected secretary of the officer's wives club, which would keep me busy for the following year. Living on the base was like living in the United States. A year had passed and I had seen nothing of this country. I could spend four years here and never see anything.

Byron's job was very demanding. He was in charge of 1,200 enlisted men and eight officers. He was on call twenty-four hours a day, seven days a week. The most we could do was drive around the immediate vicinity for a few hours to see the rice fields and country houses. I was yearning to get off the air force base and really see this foreign land. I borrowed books from the library to learn about the customs, religions, food, and festivals.

I decided I would have to take matters into my own hands. I was going to venture out to learn about Japan and its people. There was a big festival weekend coming in the town of Aomori, which could be reached by train. On Saturday morning, I packed a picnic lunch, gathered the children and Chiyo, and headed for the train station.

26

Heartbreak
Love versus Filial Duty

THE LOVELY DANCE teacher agreed to come to my house to teach me Japanese dances. I persuaded a friend to join us and the lessons started. Yoshiko-san spoke no English and my friend, Paula, and I knew just enough Japanese to get through a shopping trip in town:

"Good Afternoon," "How Much?" and "Thank you."

Yoshiko turned the music on, showed us the dance all the way through, then taught us small sections at a time until we could do the whole dance.

We looked forward to the lessons, mostly because we were fascinated with Yoshiko's graceful movements, her *kimono* sleeves flying as she whirled around, her sweet face expressing encouragement to us. She always had a different bright-colored *kimono* on, and she wore her jet-black lustrous hair combed back and up in a French twist. She was very patient with us as we tried to break the ballet habit of "toes out" and learn the Japanese method of "toes in."

Six months after we started the lessons, Paula's husband's tour of duty in Japan was finished, and they returned to the United States. Yoshiko continued to teach me and I had finally caught on and became a fast learner.

One day, Yoshiko conveyed to me (through her dictionary and Chiyo's limited help) that I had the potential to become a teacher of Japanese dance. If I worked hard for the next two and a half years and passed a difficult dance test, I could be the first foreigner to become a Japanese dance teacher.

This suggestion gave me two things to consider. The first was that I am a *foreigner*. The second, do I really want to take this challenge? Yes! Of course, I do.

Our lessons began with more intensity. Now we were dancing every day for several hours. Yoshiko spoke only Japanese, and soon, my vocabulary started to grow. Within a year, I could understand Japanese and communicate complex ideas. As I was learning the language from the spoken word, like a child does, the proper verbs, tenses, and adjectives fell into place naturally. I even learned the current slang.

Because we spent so much time together, Yoshiko and I became close friends. When we took a break in the lesson and sipped tea, we would joke and laugh together. At times, we had serious conversations and shared concerns and hopes.

One day, Yoshiko said she wanted my advice about a decision she had to make. She said she knew a boy she liked very much when she was in high school eight years ago. The feeling was mutual, and although teenagers in Japan didn't date as they do in the United States, Yoshiko and her boyfriend had an "understanding."

After graduation, Yoshiko went on to study dancing and become a well-respected teacher. The boy joined the Japanese Air Force and was a mechanic who worked on airplanes. Eight years have passed and she received a letter from him yesterday.

He wrote that his father told him it was time for him to marry, and unless he had someone he preferred to marry, the family had a wife picked out for him by a matchmaker. He wanted to know if she still loved him and if she would consider marrying him. He wanted to meet with her and talk.

Arranged marriages were the custom in Japan at that time. It was common procedure to hire a go-between when it was time for a son or daughter to marry. The go-between would consult the position of the stars on the birth dates of the prospective couples and other complex but important aspects of the individuals. Many times the bride and groom had never met before. In the present day (2010 at the time of this writing), with the Western influence, most Japanese marriages are love matches.

Yoshiko talked with her parents that night, and they warned her not to consider this proposal. There was a class system in Japan. A mechanic who works on greasy engines is no match for an accomplished professional dance instructor. Her family warned her that she would lose many students and people would talk about her behind her back. To make matters worse, her parents would not acknowledge any children born of such a marriage. They gave her permission to meet with the boy to discuss and decide, but the meeting could not be in a public place where town people would see them.

My husband was away on temporary duty for a week, so I offered my house as a meeting place. On the night of the meeting, Yoshiko arrived early looking beautiful but nervous. I sent the children to their rooms with warnings to stay there. There was a knock at the door, and when I opened it, there stood a handsome young man, also looking nervous. Yoshiko introduced us and I left them alone in the living room with some tea and snacks I had placed on the coffee table.

I stayed in the bedroom listening to music and trying to concentrate on reading a book. If this were happening in the United States, the outcome would undoubtedly be "and they lived happily ever after." But this was Yoshiko's country with its own set of standards and traditions. I couldn't advise her and I couldn't surmise what her answer would be.

At long last, I heard the front door close. I waited a few minutes, then cautiously walked down the hall to the living room. Yoshiko was standing with her back to me, facing the door.

"Yoshiko?"

"Yes."

"Did you decide?"

"Yes."

"Are you getting married?"

She turned around, her eyes filled with tears. I opened my arms and held her while her heart broke.

Yoshiko held no resentment toward her parents, and she presented a charming, happy disposition to her family and her students. After two and a half years of hard work, I passed the test and received my teacher's certificate.

Alice performing her test dance

Dance lessons

After I passed my dance test, Yoshiko and I took a trip to Kamakura to visit one of the principal dance instructors who had judged my dance. We visited the great Buddha and had our fortunes told at a shrine.

We stopped to feed a flock of birds at the park. They crowded around us while we offered the bird food. When it was all gone, the birds flew away in a hurry. I said, "They're just like people."

"Why, Okusan?" Yoshiko asked.

"They come around when you have something to give, but when you have nothing they disappear."

Yoshiko said, "No, Okusan. When you have nothing is when your true friends come."

Feeding the Birds

The Great Buddha

27

Dangerous Dewclops

LIVING QUARTERS ON Misawa Air Base were assigned to families based on a combined scale of rank and size of family. We were authorized to have a large house, but none were available when we arrived so we lived in a small trailer house.

A few months later, we were moved to Wherry Housing, which was a series of new apartment buildings. In back of these apartments, there was a collection of old airplane parts and other odd pieces of machinery. The area had a wire fence around it, but it wasn't high enough to prevent small boys from climbing over it to search for treasures.

Mothers were apprehensive about the junk pile as we knew it was a matter of time before someone got seriously hurt from the mysterious things hidden behind that fence. We warned our boys not to go in there, but the temptation was too great.

Kenny was seven years old that summer. Buz and Patty were the chatterboxes in our family. Ken was inclined to be quiet. He also had a problem pronouncing his Rs and Ls.

One day, he came in with a deep bleeding gash on his head. "What happened to you?" I asked in horror. "I got hurt with a dewclop!" he said between sobs.

"You've been playing in that junk pile again, haven't you?" Not knowing what a dewclop was, I assumed it was the technical name for a piece of machinery. I rushed him to the base hospital and the doctor sat Kenny on the examining table. "What happened to you, young man?"

Before Kenny could answer, I expressed my dissatisfaction with the Air Force for putting a junk pile next to living quarters. "He got hurt by a dewclop. Somebody has to do something about those dewclops!" I said. "Heaven only knows what else is in that pile for the boys to get into. They should build a playground instead of having hazardous material by the living quarters!"

The doctor cleaned Ken's wound, took a few stitches, and made a notation in his chart that the wound was caused by a dewclop.

When we got home, I called Buz who was playing with some boys. "I want you to show me where those dewclops are. Your brother got badly hurt with one."

"Mom, we were throwing dirt clods at each other. He got hit with a *dirt clod!*"

Fifty years later, when I was recalling the incident, Ken told me he knew he had pronounced it wrong at the time, but he was really embarrassed for me when *I* started calling it a dewclop.

Several months later, we moved into our permanent quarters: a house with four and a half bedrooms, three bathrooms, and plenty of living space.

Ken was in the kitchen watching me make supper when Patty and Buz came in from play.

He dashed into the living room and said, "I know what we're having for supper. It starts with a W."

His siblings started to guess. "Waffles?"

"Uh uh."

"Weiners?"

"Uh uh. Guess again."

"Watermelon?"

"Waldorf salad?"

"Walnuts?

"Nope. Give up?"

"Yeah."

"Wavioli" (ravioli).

28

Chiyo

I HAVE MADE many attempts to write a chapter about Chiyo, but have failed each time.

She was our beloved housemaid during the four years we lived in Japan. There are so many complex ways to describe her, none of which would give full credit to her personality.

She was sweet, mild mannered, and soft-spoken. But I have seen her shout orders to a group of Japanese workmen while swatting them with a broom.

She had a happy disposition, working steadily and efficiently all day with no display of stress. But I could sense, in one minute, her silent grief one day. I had come home with bags of groceries and said, "Hi, Chiyo!" Chiyo answered, "Hi," and started unpacking the bags. There was an absence of something in that kitchen. Her lively spirit was gone.

I asked, "Chiyo? Is something wrong?" She hesitated and then forced a smile and said, "My husband die. Terry (her daughter) now telephone."

"Oh, Chiyo. I'm so sorry. I didn't know he was sick. Why didn't you tell me?"

"December, Christmas time busy for your family. Parties, dinners."

"But, Chiyo, we would have done the work ourselves. Get your things. I'll drive you home right now."

"No, Patty-san have party tonight." Patty was having her first boy-girl party. It was New Year's Eve. I assured Chiyo we could handle everything by ourselves. I drove her home and told her to take the month of January off with pay.

She was a grandmother to our children, always delighting in their antics and accomplishments. The children loved her dearly and were eager to show her their drawings, their judo maneuvers, a new dance or song. She gave them her total attention when they had something to tell her. Many times in a day, one of the children would say, "Chiyo—watch this!" or "Chiyo, guess what!" and she would stop and smile lovingly while she listened.

Since I can't describe Chiyo in a chapter, she will pop up in other stories about our life in Japan. She will also appear in the "Letters from Japan" section. I'm sure her spirit will invade the entire segment about Japan, and you will get to know and love her too.

29

The Bar Girl, the Communists, and Chiyo's Rules

I WAS IN a panic. Patty had grown chubby during the past few months, and none of the girls' clothes in the BX (base exchange) would fit her. Summer of 1959 was ending. School would start in two weeks and Patty had nothing to wear.

I could sew quite well, but there were no patterns available to buy. Some families hired seamstresses. Japanese seamstresses made their own patterns. All you had to do was show them a picture in a magazine, and they could duplicate it perfectly.

I went to the base employment office, which was called the labor office. I was told there was a long waiting list for a seamstress. "How long? School starts in two weeks!"

They told me it could be as long as two years before one was available.

Determined to find a seamstress, I left the base and walked downtown. Surely, the Japanese people would have an employment office of their own. I stopped someone on the street and asked where the labor office was. He pointed to a building that had a red flag hanging outside.

My spirits brightened and I entered the building. The walls had large posters of coal miners. There were three Japanese men standing behind a long desk who looked at me curiously as I approached them. I found out much later that I was not in an employment office. I was in the local communist headquarters.

"I'm looking for a seamstress," I said. "Do you have any available?" The men put their heads together and discussed this. Finally, the one who could speak a little English asked, "You want a *seamstress?*"

"Yes, I need one to sew school clothes for my daughter."

They talked with each other at great length while I waited expectantly. One of the men would make a suggestion and the others would shake their heads no. I thought it was strange that they didn't look through their files, but figured since it was a small town, they didn't need to keep records. After much discussion, they picked up the phone and started making calls. Finally, the man beckoned to me and said, "She be at main gate tomorrow eight o'clock. Name Michiko."

I thanked him, and they all smiled and bowed. Happily, I shopped in the town for dress material and was relieved that the problem had been solved.

At eight o'clock the next morning, I drove to the main gate to look for Michiko. The only person that was waiting outside the gate was a girl who wore a very short miniskirt, high heels, and a revealing blouse. Her black hair hung loose down to her waist, and she wore heavy makeup. She was certainly not the typical sweet-looking Japanese girl I expected.

I approached her and said, "Michiko?" She nodded yes. I asked, "Can you sew?" She nodded yes. So I said, "Get in the car."

When we arrived at our house, Chiyo opened the door and looked Michiko up and down, her arms folded across her chest. Then she looked at me as if to say, "Are you out of your mind?" I said, "Chiyo, this is Michiko. She is going to sew clothes for Patty." I never saw Chiyo so hostile. We had to wiggle our way past her to get in.

I had set up my sewing machine in the dining room, and I showed Michiko pictures of clothes in a magazine. She measured Patty and then went about the business of sewing.

At noon, Byron came home for lunch and I made sandwiches for everyone. I invited Michiko to have lunch with us, and she sat at the dining room table while I introduced her to Byron and the children. She started to chat with us, and I noticed she spoke English fairly well. Byron asked her a few questions and she talked with him at great length.

Chiyo was in the kitchen noisily banging pots and pans.

Later in the afternoon, Michiko asked me where the bathroom was and I showed her. As soon as Michiko entered the bathroom, Chiyo came and stood by the closed door with a can of Lysol in her hand. It didn't take much imagination to realize that Chiyo was extremely upset with the situation. Gone was her cheerful smile and pleasant singing. Dead silence reigned, punctuated occasionally by a slamming drawer.

Five o'clock was approaching and Chiyo came to me and asked, "She come back tomorrow?" I said, "Yes, Chiyo. Patty needs clothes for school. She'll be here for quite a while."

Her face took on the expression of a marine sergeant, and she turned to confront Michiko in the dining room. Chiyo's voice changed from her sweet singsong soprano to a deep-pitched growl as she talked to Michiko. I heard her say something about lunch (*obento*) and toilet (*benjo*). She also mentioned "Papa-san" several times. A subdued Michiko left the house at five o'clock.

The next morning, Michiko arrived wearing a cotton blouse, a skirt that covered her knees, and flat shoes. Her hair was pulled up into a bun and she wore no makeup.

She carried a *furoshiki* (a large scarf tied in four corners to form a pouch) that had her lunch inside. She went right to work at the sewing machine, and when the family gathered for lunch, she disappeared into the kitchen with her own lunch.

Apparently, Chiyo's orders included staying away from Papa-san because she kept her eyes lowered and did not speak when Byron was in the room. I also noticed Chiyo had told her to use the small powder room, not the large bathroom the family uses.

Patty's first dress turned out perfect. I found several more pictures for Michiko to copy. I had a feeling Michiko was going to be around for a long time. The BX had very few selections for women's clothes, and I started searching the magazines for clothes for myself. My friends were impressed with her work and asked if they could borrow her for special clothes. Michiko worked in our house for a year, making clothes for Patty and Barbara. She made a complete wardrobe for me.

When she had filled our closets and I couldn't think of any more clothes for her to make, she had her pick of my friends who were clamoring for her. She was assured of a job for years.

From the day Chiyo laid down the rules and Michiko had acquiesced, a state of harmony existed between them. Chiyo and Michiko spoke to each other within the boundaries of Japanese manners, but never to the extent of familiarity. Chiyo's cheerful spirit returned and filled our house with love and song.

Perhaps we contributed to Michiko's successful career as a seamstress, which led to her rejection of the previous way she made a living. She arrived in our lives at a crucial time. Since she was very young (about eighteen), maybe we arrived in her life at a pivotal time.

And although I sought help from the officials in communist headquarters, they did their best to find someone for me. They helped me when I needed help and I am grateful to them. My husband worked in Security Service, serving his country with a very high security clearance, keeping a close watch on developments in Communist Russia. He never asked me where I found Michiko and I didn't tell him.

Addendum: The communist party in Japan in the late 1950s was a very small minority group. In the town of Misawa, there were about twenty members. Once a year, they notified base headquarters that a demonstration would take place at a specified date and time. Extra guards were placed at the main gate on the appointed day. Fearful air force wives herded their children into their living quarters and locked the doors

When the hour arrived, a few men quietly walked up to the gate carrying signs. Then they retreated and returned to their homes. There were no crowds, no shouting, and certainly no hateful expressions. The guards dispersed, wives unlocked their doors, and the children happily returned to their play outdoors.

30

Tranquility
The Essence of Japan

B YRON HAD BEEN working seven days a week for three months. Finally, the urgency for all those hours of work subsided, and we were able to plan for a relaxing getaway weekend.

I had read about a hot springs inn by a lake in the mountains. It was in a remote location. No towns or villages were anywhere near it and the road was not paved. We decided to try it and four other couples wanted to join us.

Chiyo stayed with the children, and we led the way with our car while the other couples followed in two cars. The road up the mountain was winding and treacherous at times. As we drove around a curve, we came upon a gorgeous waterfall. We had to get out to see it in all its glory. The water was falling from such a great height; we stood mesmerized, reluctant to leave the peace we felt.

After a long and dusty drive, we arrived at the inn. We were greeted at the door by several beautiful Japanese ladies, and each of us was given a *yukata* (cotton *kimono*) to wear. They ushered us to a large room that, at bedtime, would be divided into four rooms by sliding doors.

Tea and a light lunch were served to us. We were told to put the *yukatas* on and wear them while we were there for the weekend, even if we went outdoors for walks. They showed us where the hot springs bath was and told us we could go there at any time and as many times as we desired.

We all changed into our *yukatas* and went our separate ways. Byron and I went outdoors and walked on a trail that led to the lake. It was late September, a pleasantly warm day, and leaves were just starting to turn color. We came to a clearing, and there before us was a scene of tranquility I will never forget. The lake was still, not a ripple disturbed its surface. Surrounding the lake were tall trees that were reflected in the mirrorlike water. Not a sound was heard. No talking. No music. Not even a bird. We felt like we were in a primeval land. The beauty and peace held us silent and motionless. We hadn't expected such a hallowed sanctuary.

I don't know how long we were held captive in this exquisite atmosphere, but we left it reluctantly and joined the group back at the inn.

The men decided they were going to soak in the hot springs. It was in a large enclosed area and was open to both men and women. We asked our hostesses if there was a smaller private bath that the women in our group could go to, and she led us to a room that was just perfect for the five of us.

We were instructed to disrobe completely, wash with soap and water, and rinse with the water that was contained in wooden buckets. After we were thoroughly clean, we could descend into the steaming pool of water and relax.

We followed instructions and started to enter the pool. It was HOT! The only way to do it was to just go in all at once. The water came up to our necks when we were standing up. I felt like a lobster being prepared for someone's dinner. After a few minutes, we became acclimated to the water temperature and found it quite soothing and relaxing.

Just as we decided it was time to get out, the door opened and a little old man entered the room. We looked at each other, trying to decide what to do. We didn't want to get out, naked as we were, so we just stayed in the water.

The man removed his *yukata*, washed himself, and entered the pool, discretely carrying his washcloth, not once looking our way. Once he was in the pool, there was no way to avoid the fact that we were in there with him. He kept his eyes lowered and bowed to us. We bowed back, which was difficult because we were already in water up to our necks.

Eventually, the man got out, dressed himself, and left quietly. We escaped from the water, our bodies red from the heat, put our *yukatas* on, and hurried to our room. The men were already there enjoying cold beer and asked, "What kept you so long?"

Dinner was prepared on a small charcoal *hibachi* on the table we sat around. The Japanese ladies made a stir-fry entrée and served it with rice, soup, pickles, and fruit. We were all in a peaceful mood after dinner and talked quietly. A gentle breeze came through an open sliding door.

After a while, we heard a *samisen* being strummed and someone singing softly. We started to sing some American songs. Our energy returned, and we all stood up and danced the "Coal Miner's Dance," a simple Japanese dance that all Americans learn quickly.

There was a quiet knock at our rice paper door. We wondered if we were being too loud. When we opened it, a Japanese man smiled and motioned for us to come across the hall to their party. Their *shoji* door was open and we could see some Japanese ladies in gorgeous *kimonos*: one played a *samisen*, one was dancing, and another was pouring *sake* (rice wine) for the men.

We joined them. Our men were served rice wine. We women declined. I had experienced the effects of *sake* once before and didn't want to repeat that disaster.

We drank sodas and the Japanese ladies taught us some dances. Soon the men were "old buddies," singing together and laughing.

Byron was sitting with a man who had been a physician in the Japanese army. Fourteen years ago, they had been mortal enemies. On this night, they had their arms around each other, singing and talking, each trying to communicate in the other's language, and they were comrades.

This was a significant moment. I reached for my camera and captured it.

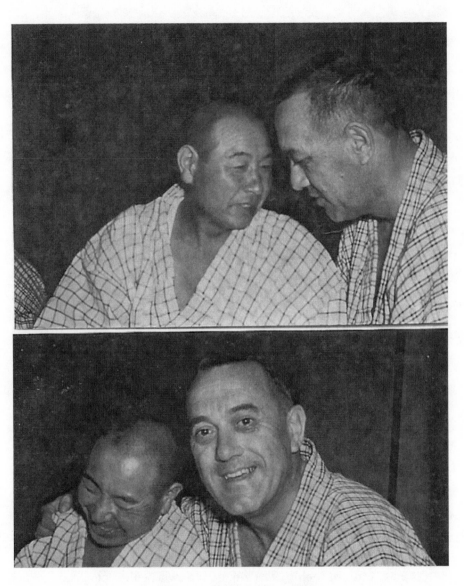

Formerly foes, now friends

31

Nobu-chan
A Samurai Descendant

T HE FOLLOWING ADVENTURE is copied from a letter I wrote
to my father and sister.

August 13, 1959

Dear folks,

Last Thursday, I took a trip to Aomori with Chiyo and the
children. It's a city about two hours from here by train. I've
waited all summer for Byron to take us somewhere on a
weekend, but he has been too busy at work. I decided to try
it on my own if I was going to see anything of Japan. Aomori
was having a huge Nebuta Festival and I wanted to see it.

Well, the night before our trip, I made fourteen peanut butter
and jelly sandwiches and put them in the refrigerator. My kids
won't eat anything but peanut butter and jelly for lunch except
Patty who got sophisticated on me and switched to bologna.

We headed for the railroad station the next morning, Chiyo
carrying Barbara on her back and me toting the picnic basket.
Unfortunately, I had forgotten to put the sandwiches in it. I
didn't realize this until much later.

Terry (Chiyo's daughter) told me it was more fun to go third-class and cheaper too. She said, "Everyone who rides second-class is 'stuck up.' Nobody talks, just sit there with their nose in the air. Third-class more better. Everybody friendly. Everybody talks. Have a lot of fun." So I bought third-class tickets, hoping to make some friends during the ride.

Third-class was crowded with humanity. Some people had chickens in crates. Some had produce in large baskets on their backs. There was not a seat for any of us to sit down, so we stood up for the entire two hours and nobody talked to me.

I found out there is no first-class. That's just for the emperor.

We arrived, hot and thirsty, in Aomori. The city was filled with people who had come from all over the countryside for the Nebuta Festival. Most of them had never seen Americans before.

We looked around the stores a while and then Chiyo took us on a bus ride out to the beach. This was my first time at a Japanese beach. Their beach wear is at a minimum, especially the boys and men. They wear something like a jockstrap. The boys under six just don't wear anything at all. Girls up to about twelve just wear their underpants.

We were sitting down on the sand watching the sights when I noticed some people hiding behind a rock, taking pictures of us. Then they started inching their way toward us, and before I knew it, there was a circle of black-haired, black-eyed people around me as far as I could see. I'm not exaggerating when I say there were at least one hundred people packed in a circle around us. We started to walk to a different place and the whole circle moved. It must have looked funny from an airplane.

From somewhere in the crowd, I heard a voice asking, "Where do you come from?" There was a boy, about sixteen or seventeen years old, speaking to us. He told us he was a school boy on a holiday and he speaks English because he is studying English in school. His father is a city official.

He offered to be our guide for the day since this was our first visit to Aomori. He said, "I will take you someplace quiet." That sounded like a good idea to me at the time. We were packed between so many people, if I had fainted, I couldn't have fallen down.

He led us away from the beach, but the one hundred followers came with us. At one point, Barbara wandered away from us and the crowd left us to follow Barbara. Then I realized these people were fascinated with Barbara. I wish you could have seen it. There was two-year-old Barbara with her bouncing blond curls, unaware that she was leading a parade that stretched the length of the beach. Chiyo told me the people were saying, "She looks like a doll."

Well, our newfound friend told us this "someplace quiet" was only a short walk, but it lasted an hour. We were way out in the country, off the beaten path. Chiyo was carrying Barbara on her back and I was lugging a picnic basket that got surprisingly heavy for not having any sandwiches in it.

My legs were aching, the kids were moaning, and the sun beat down on us as we got farther and farther into nowhere. We finally got there. It was a cemetery. I dropped exhausted in the shade of a tomb. The atmosphere in the cemetery was cheerful. People were having picnics, and some children were running around with butterfly nets, chasing butterflies over the graves.

While I sat there, catching my breath, Kenny was up in a tree trying to recover his toy parachute and the boy (Nobu-chan) told me about himself. His grandfather and all his ancestors way back were *samurai*. That was the highest class of people there was in Japan besides the emperor's family. The *samurai* no longer rule the territories, but the people still have respect for their descendants.

Nobu-chan told me he is very interested in America and wants to go there to study. He's also very interested in American folk songs. At his request, I joined him in singing "Carry Me Back to Old Viginny" and "Swanee River." Then I listened politely while he recited the entire Gettysburg Address.

We went back to the city by bus, which was packed with people going to the festival.

During the bus ride, Nobu-chan sang every American folk song he knew.

When we got back to Aomori, we ate in a restaurant. Chiyo ordered for us as they had no menus in English. I'm not sure what we ate, but it was delicious. The children were better at eating with chopsticks than I was.

The Nebuta Festival was at 8:30 that night. This festival is over a thousand years old. It was led by a big parade of dancers in beautiful kimonos and huge paper dragons with lights inside. While we stood watching the ancient dances to the strange rhythm of drums and flutes, I felt like I was in another world in another time.

Nobu-chan walked with us to the train station and saw us off, running alongside our window until the train was too fast. I just received a letter from him today in which he accepts my invitation to visit us and will come in October.

Nobu-chan with Buz

32

A Samurai Family

BEFORE WE BOARDED the train in Aomori to go home, Nobu-chan gave us a card with his name and address. He said he would like to visit us. I wrote to him, and a few weeks later, he arrived by train for a visit.

He carried a translation dictionary with him and referred to it many times during our conversations. His English was academic. He spoke English as it was taught in high school by teachers who didn't speak English. Whenever there was a lull in the conversation, he would sing an American folk song for our entertainment. At the end of his visit, he invited us to visit his town the following Saturday.

Byron and I left the children home with Chiyo and rode the train to a very small country village. It was a very remote country village. Nobu-chan met us at the station and proudly ushered us to a taxi. It was the only car in the town. The only other vehicles with wheels were carts pulled by dogs or old women.

We rode along like royalty for about half a block until the car stopped dead. The embarrassed taxi driver got out and fiddled around with the engine, kicked at it, threatened it, but nothing seemed to persuade the stubborn car, so we got out and walked to Nobu-chan's house, waving to all the people who were in the doorways of their small houses bowing and waving to us.

At Nobu-chan's house, we removed our shoes and walked in our stocking feet down a polished hallway to a room with paper sliding doors. The floor in the room was covered with thick straw mats (*tatami*) and was wonderfully resilient. I bounced as I walked on it. Nobu-chan placed large pillows on the floor for us to kneel on, and we sat around a low table. On top of the table was a small clay pot with charcoal burning in it.

Japanese houses have no clutter or excess furniture. The room we were in was sparse. It had the four walls (one of which was the sliding paper door), the *tatami* floor, and the pillows that we sat on. There was one focal point of décor: an alcove with a small table that held a flower arrangement. On the wall behind the flower arrangement was a long hanging scroll displaying beautiful artwork. That was called the *tokonoma*. Byron was directed to sit in front of the *tokonoma* or place of honor. Nobu-chan told us the scroll was two hundred years old and had belonged to his great-great-grandfather who was a *samurai*.

After a few minutes, Nobu-chan clapped his hands one time and called, "*Kasan*." His mother appeared, deftly opening the sliding doors and entering on her knees, bowing rapidly to us and chattering pleasantly as she carried in trays of food beautifully arranged in lovely dishes.

She was a tiny, lovable woman who has had eight children, most of them grown up now. You could tell by looking at her pixie face and twinkling eyes that she would be fun to be with. The dinner she served us consisted of the following:

Yo-kan—maroon-colored jellylike cubes made of compressed sweet bean paste

Sushi—vinegar rice balls with thin slices of raw fish

Kaki—persimmons

Ocha—green tea

Miso-shiru—bean paste soup with bean curd

Nobu-chan's father joined us for dinner. He wasn't at all what I expected as a descendant of a *samurai*. He was a tiny, unassuming man with a shy smile. He had an important job in Aomori in the attorney general's office.

After dinner, we went out to an apple orchard and picked several baskets of apples to take home with us. Nobu-chan's mother and I became good friends. She doesn't speak English and yet we seemed to understand each other. She and I had a grand time climbing ladders and picking apples.

We were unaware that Nobu-chan had declared this a special day for the village and the school. This was the first time any Americans had visited the town. That explained why all the people were standing outside their houses when we arrived.

The high school was opened especially for us. When we arrived at the school, the principal and all the teachers were waiting on the steps, bowing to us. Before we entered, we removed our shoes as we noticed everyone else did.

We were led to each classroom where exhibits of the students' work were on display. All the high school boys and girls were dressed in their uniforms, standing by their displays. We had to pose for pictures in every room.

Then we were taken into the principal's office. We sat at a table while some girls served us *shiruko* (sweet bean soup) that was made by the girls in the home economics class.

With students and teachers in Nobu-chan's school

When it was time for us to leave, the taxi arrived at Nobu-chan's house. The proud taxi driver, all smiles, was waiting to drive us to the train. We rode for a half a block and the taxi stopped.

This time, the taxi driver was really mad. He jerked up the hood of the car, threatened the engine with his fist, and although he spoke only Japanese, even I could perceive he was using some pretty abusive language.

He begged us to wait. I could see he was embarrassed, but we had only a few minutes to catch the train, so we left him talking to his engine while we ran for the train.

We made quite a procession running through town. Nobu-chan, his mother and father, Byron and I, all hanging on to baskets of apples while the town people stood in the doorways of their shops and bowed *sayonara* to us. Nobu-chan's mother managed to bow back to them without missing a step, but all I could manage was to duck my head a couple of times.

Someone had presented Byron with a branch from an apple tree. It had five apples on it and symbolized something about fertility. As he ran, the apples dropped off, one by one.

When we arrived at the station, all he had was a withered branch left, which is just as well. Four children in our family are plenty.

As we pulled out of the station, Nobu-chan's mother ran alongside the train by our window, promising to come and see me. Her kimono sleeves fluttered like a butterfly.

Her mischievous eyes were full of friendship.

One month later, Nobu-chan's family came to our house for a visit. As we sat down to dinner, each of them took out their own chopsticks instead of using the silverware at their place. I marveled at how skillful they were. There was a moment when I was concerned about how they could deal with the Jell-O fruit salad, but Nobu-chan's mother used her chopsticks to cut small squares in the Jell-O and the rest of her family followed suit.

Nobu-chan's mother

33

A Christmas Surprise

SOMETIME DURING OUR second year in Japan, I became fascinated with the *samisen*; a Japanese stringed instrument. A very versatile instrument, it was used during *kabuki* dramas to set moods from tenderness to terror. It was also used to furnish music during dance recitals. Geishas were accomplished at playing the *samisen*.

The body of the *samisen* was square and box shaped. It had a long neck and three strings made of twisted silk, each of different thicknesses to produce higher and lower pitches. It was played with a plectrum.

I asked my dance teacher if she would introduce me to the elderly lady who played the *samisen* at our local dance recitals. I never knew her name, but I called her Sensei (teacher). She started coming to my house once a week to teach me how to play. She brought an extra *samisen* for me to use during the lessons.

When she arrived, I placed two large *zabuton* pillows on the floor, and we kneeled on them, facing each other. Sensei would play for a few minutes while I watched the placement of her fingers on the neck and the string she plucked. Then she motioned for me to imitate her. We went over and over the segment until I had learned it. Then we continued on. While we played, Sensei sang. I never tried to learn to sing along. It was hard enough to learn to play by this rote method.

Sometimes, while we were playing, my husband came home for lunch and listened to us.

After about ninety minutes, Sensei bowed, packed up her instruments, and left. Byron asked me how I could kneel for so long without shifting. It didn't seem to bother me. I was concentrating on learning and felt no discomfort.

Christmas was coming soon. While we were shopping in the base exchange for gifts for the children, I passed by a little nook that sold Japanese artifacts. Displayed on the wall was a beautiful *samisen* with red-and-gold trimming. I pointed it out to Byron, and he gave it a cursory glance.

The week before Christmas I noticed a strange box in our closet. It was sealed so I couldn't peek, but I told Sensei that I might be getting a *samisen* for Christmas. Her English was very limited, but she urged me to open the box so she could inspect it. I told her I couldn't—it was a surprise.

Sure enough, Christmas morning came and that box was wrapped and under the tree with my name on it. It was the *samisen* from the base exchange. When Sensei arrived for our next lesson, she was curious to know if that box really contained a *samisen*. I nodded and proudly brought it forth for her to see.

Her face puckered up and a deep frown covered her usually serene forehead. "*Doko?*" she asked. Where? She called Chiyo into the room and they talked. Chiyo turned to me and asked, "Papa-san buy BX?"

"Yes, he bought it at the base exchange."

Chiyo said, "Sensei say we go to BX! Bad *samisen*!"

The base exchange was strictly for use by American servicemen and their families. It carried American-made goods, clothes, cooking utensils, cigarettes, towels, etc. Sensei didn't have a pass to get in, but she was still frowning and looked determined, so I packed her in the car, still holding on to my *samisen*, and we drove to the BX. Somehow we slipped in without being noticed. I don't know how as Sensei was dressed in traditional *kimono*. We arrived at the Japanese concession, and Sensei blasted the young Japanese salesman. With gestures and tone of voice, Sensei made everyone around us aware of how dissatisfied she was with this purchase.

The young man backed up and with an apologetic and respectful attitude gave her an explanation. Someone stepped in to translate for me.

"Look at that warped neck! How do you think she is going to play it with a neck like that?"

"Well, I'm sorry, but I didn't know she was going to *play* it!"

"What did you *think* she was going to do with a *samisen*?"

"Well, I thought she was going to hang it on a wall as a decoration!"

Nobody translated what the Sensei said to that. It ended up with the young salesman assuring me that he would have a number one excellent *samisen* for me in two days.

We left after Sensei let him know she was going to examine the new one carefully.

The next *samisen* passed inspection with flying colors and our lessons took off. Now that I could practice between lessons, we were making progress. Sensei started coming twice a week, then three times a week. I was learning long pieces, and soon I joined her at dance recitals, providing music for the dancers.

Months later, I was in a department store in Tokyo. I walked around the music department and came across music books for the *samisen*. I bought several and showed them to my Sensei. "Why didn't you tell me there were music books for the *samisen*? It would have been so much easier for me to learn."

She shrugged and said she thought I learned just fine without the books.

Christmas samisen

34

Volunteer Chauffeur

BYRON WAS ABLE to get away from work for four days and our whole family boarded the train for the twelve-hour ride to Tokyo. We stayed at the Ueno Hotel in Tokyo overnight and awoke the next morning, eager to start our sightseeing adventure.

After breakfast in the dining room, we gathered in the lobby to hail a taxi at the entrance.

What we saw was a long line of people with the same idea. Looking out the front door, we saw a massive rainstorm. The drive from the street to the hotel's front door was shaped like a horseshoe, and taxis were lined up waiting for their turn at the door.

As soon as a taxi rolled to a stop, the doorman, armed with a large umbrella, opened the taxi door and guided each group, in turn, into the taxi. After waiting patiently, we were in front of the line, and when the next car drove up, someone got out of the car and we rushed to get in, dodging the raindrops. The car was small and there were six of us, so I told the boys to run around the car and get in the front seat with the driver.

Byron said, "Take us to Tokyo Tower, please," and the driver said, "*Hai,*" which means yes. We settled back, watching the pedestrians hurrying along sidewalks, trying in vain to keep dry. We had planned to do many things this day, and we hoped the rain would let up by afternoon when we went to the zoo. Tokyo Tower was first on our list. It was a new structure and a great tourist attraction. At the very top, you could see the entire city of Tokyo from all angles. On the way down to the ground floor, there were specialty shops and restaurants.

After a while, I looked toward the front of the taxi to see how much the meter was reading, but I couldn't see a meter. I noticed the driver wasn't wearing a uniform or taxi driver's hat. I turned to Byron and whispered, "I don't think this is a taxi." He came to the same conclusion, tapped the driver on the back, and said, "This isn't a taxi, is it?" The driver said, "*Hai,*" meaning "Yes, you are right. This isn't a taxi." It isn't polite in Japan to say no to someone. Apparently, he had dropped off a friend at the hotel, and we all jumped into his car.

We said, "We're so sorry. Stop the car and we'll get out and find a taxi." The man said, "No, I take you to Tokyo Tower. Almost there." We were embarrassed and offered to pay the man when we arrived at our destination. He refused payment and said it was his pleasure. He also said, "I wait for you. I take you to next place when you finish here."

We thanked him but told him to leave because we would probably be at Tokyo Tower a long time.

We took the elevator to the top of the tower, took pictures from each side, and I could see the man's car still parked where we left him. Each time we went down a floor, we looked out a window and he was still there. We tried to take our time, hoping he would get discouraged and go away, but he remained steadfast. The sun came out and the children were anxious to go to the zoo.

The man smiled and opened his car doors when he saw us come out. "Where you go now?" he asked. The children said, "The zoo," and off we went. I told him he shouldn't have waited for us, and he said he liked to hear our family speak English. He wanted to show us the sights of the city.

After the zoo, we went to the Takarazuka Theater and saw a magnificent show. The first half was American style. There were our popular songs, costumes, and dances just like Radio City Music Hall. The second half was Japanese songs and beautiful dances. The scenery was gorgeous. The theater was grand and luxurious.

We left the theater and piled into our friend's waiting car. Arriving at Ueno Hotel, he opened the car doors and four sleepy children shuffled into the hotel as we thanked our willing guide. I don't think I would ever find someone like that in any country. I have never forgotten him and his kindness.

35

Snowbound

THE WEEKEND STARTED out innocently enough. We looked forward to a pleasant, relaxing Saturday, January 9, 1960.

In the afternoon, we received a phone call from Nobu-chan. He was at the train station and announced that he was here to visit us for two days. Byron drove to the station to bring him home. He arrived in the house with his suitcase, a trumpet, and his ever-present dictionary.

Patty, Buz, and Kenny had an early supper and rode the bus to the base theater to see a movie. We had invited friends over for dinner, so we set an extra place for Nobu-chan and he occupied himself looking up words that we were using during our conversations with our friends.

Facing the dining room windows, I noticed large snowflakes coming down. It was a beautiful sight. We had just finished dessert when the children blasted through the front door, covered with snow, stomping their feet. "What are you doing home so early?" we asked. "They stopped the movie and announced that we had to leave immediately. The buses were going to stop running because of the snow. We caught the last bus home!"

We rushed to the door and looked out into the night. Snow was piling up fast. We turned on the radio and heard warnings that a mammoth snowstorm was upon us. We were all to go to our homes immediately. We bid good-bye to our guests and settled in for the night.

The next morning, we awoke to find the snow had completely covered our house during the night. Our house was in a valley. There were about twenty concrete stairs from our front door up to the sidewalk and street level. The snow was up to our roof gutters!

It was at this moment that Nobu-chan decided to entertain us with his singing rendition of "Carry Me Back to Old Virginny" and "Old Black Joe."

Meanwhile, Byron was trying to figure out how we could shovel our way out of this mess. We had two shovels, but since the snow was way over our heads, there was no way to throw the snow up. We had to tunnel our way out. We shoveled snow into buckets and dumped the snow into the bathtubs, toilets, and sinks. Byron and I worked as a team, then Patty and Buz took over for a while. Ken and Byron took a shift and Nobu-chan played military marches on his trumpet. He would start playing, make a mistake, and start all over.

This went on for most of the afternoon until Byron stood in front of Nobu-chan, extended the shovel, and said, "Your turn!" Nobu-chan interrupted his trumpet recital and looked at the shovel with surprise.

"We do not shovel!" he said.

"What do you mean 'we'?"

"*Samurai* do not shovel!"

Byron's exhausted body took a threatening stance, so I grabbed the shovel and offered to take Nobu-chan's picture shoveling snow. That appealed to Nobu-chan, and he donned his hat, coat, and boots and went outside with the shovel. Byron looked at me, bewildered. "How did you do that?" he whispered.

I took a whole roll of film of Nobu-chan shoveling snow in different poses while Byron stretched out in an armchair with a cup of coffee. The radio kept us up-to-date on the latest developments. There was no let-up from the snow and no speculation as to when it would end. All the air force base services and offices were closed. The base was under Disaster Control Command.

We were ordered to stay in our homes. If we ran out of food, we were to use the food in our "ready kits." Those were kits each family had in case the base was bombed or attacked. We had enough canned food in our emergency kits to last three days for each member of the family.

All transportation had stopped. There were no buses. Trains were not running. That meant Nobu-chan couldn't go home even if we could dig our way out. The commissary was closed, so nobody could buy groceries, even if they could get to the commissary.

Hours turned into days and days into a week. Nobu-chan, feeling confined and in the need for exercise, did handsprings up and down the long hall that led to the bedrooms and bathrooms. When he was in a mood to instruct us, he would recite the Preamble to the Constitution or the Gettysburg Address. Occasionally, when he tired of American folk songs, he entertained us with Elvis Presley songs. His favorite one was "Love Me Tender."

A new game developed between Byron and Nobu-chan that I watched with great interest since I was also feeling housebound and in need of diversion. Nobu-chan wore a heavy quilted *kimono* and the house temperature was too high for him. When perspiration started running down his face, he would sneak around and turn off all the radiators.

About an hour later, Byron would put down the book he was reading and complain of having chills. "What's the matter?" he'd say. "Has the heat gone off? Oh, the radiators are all turned off!" And he'd turn them all on full blast.

This game was repeated frequently. It kept my mind off the snow and the dwindling groceries. Buz and Kenny, who were both taking judo lessons, had occasional judo matches in the living room. Nobu-chan found it easier to communicate by writing notes than by looking up words in his dictionary, so we corresponded frequently. He wrote a history of his great-great-grandfather and the castle he lived in, the feudal wars he fought, etc.

On the fourth day, a ski patrol was formed to deliver milk to families that had babies.

One of my friends was in her last month of pregnancy. I called her to see how she was. She said, "Oh, I'm fine! Don't worry about me, I'm not due for three more weeks and I'm always late anyway."

Two hours after that conversation, her water broke and her husband and a neighbor shoveled frantically to clear a path for her in the blinding snowstorm. The emergency service sent a "weasel," which is similar to a tank, to take her to the hospital. She arrived at the hospital at 1:00 a.m. and had the baby at 2:00 a.m. Her fourth girl.

Nobu-chan took his daily baths. The first time he came out of the bathroom after his bath, the floor had about two inches of water on it. I had to mop it up. I assumed he had fallen asleep in the tub with the water running and it overflowed. The second time, I got tired of mopping and asked him why the floor was so wet. He explained that Japanese people wash themselves with soap while standing on the floor outside of the tub. Then they take a bucket and pour water over themselves to rinse the soap off. That takes about four buckets of water. Then they get into the hot tub and soak.

I explained that American bathrooms don't have a floor drain, so he will have to take a bath like Americans do—in the tub.

Seven days passed. We heard Nobu-chan's trumpet repertoire over and over. His handsprings up and down the hall became routine, and I no longer wondered if he was going to break his back or head. I had memorized the Gettysburg Address in junior high school, but now it was embedded permanently in my brain. The radiator game had become old, and we were running out of paper for Nobu-chan to write his notes on.

It was Saturday again, and as I went to the kitchen to see what I could scrape together for breakfast, I heard a bus go past our house. I turned on the radio and announcements were flowing. The commissary was open. The roads were plowed. Trains were running!

"Nobu-chan. You can go home!" Nobu-chan gathered his belongings. Someone was plowing the rest of our concrete steps up to the sidewalk. The snow had stopped.

As Nobu-chan turned toward me to say good-bye, he handed me his last note. I closed the door behind him and opened the note. It said, "I will try to come back next month."

The schools opened on Monday. That ended the children's weeklong vacation. Kenny had an extra two days though. The snow was fifty-two inches high all over the base, and the children had to be at least fifty-two inches tall. Kenny was only forty-eight inches, so he got to stay home a little longer.

Nobu-chan kept in touch with us for the next three years, sending us pictures of himself and his friends on school holidays. The letters he wrote to me always started with "Dear Little Mother." Eventually, Nobu-chan graduated and started working. He used me as a reference, and I gave high praises when prospective employers asked for a reference. He visited us several more times, and although he had grown up and deserved to be called Nobu-san, he will always be Nobu-chan to me. *Chan* is a title given to children. *San* is the honorary title given to an adult. It is similar to our *sir* or *mister*.

We lost touch when we moved back to the United States. I often wonder if he ever visited our country.

Nobu-chan grows up

36

Kindness Has No Borders

M Y HUSBAND HAD scheduled a three-day series of meetings in Tokyo. Chiyo agreed to stay at our house and take care of the children, so I took this opportunity to go with him and do some sightseeing and shopping while he was at the meetings.

On the first day, I went to an afternoon performance at a Kabuki theater. I find it difficult to compare Kabuki with anything we have in the United States or Europe. The stage scenery is a masterpiece of art and the scenery changes are magical. So smoothly and discretely are the changes made, you are completely unaware of it. The costumes are magnificent. The plays run the gamut of love, pathos, filial duty, treachery, rivalry, and honor. I would compare Kabuki with opera except the spoken word is substituted for the singing.

I bought a ticket for the front row and was thrilled to be so close to the action. I was so impressed with the glorious atmosphere of this style of theater, I bought a ticket for the following day's matinee. There is a different play each day.

By the third day, I had spent quite a bit of money on front-row seats and shopping on the Ginza, but I was determined to see another Kabuki show. So I bought a ticket with the money I had left. It was way in the back of the balcony.

I arrived early and the show wouldn't start for an hour, so I went to a coffee shop across the street. It was crowded, and as is the custom, people sit at tables with strangers when it is crowded. I was sitting alone when a man and his son took the seats across from me. The son appeared to be a university student, and from their conversation with each other, I learned he was on a short holiday and his father was treating him to an outing.

"So how are your studies going?" he asked his son.

"They are fine."

"Are you getting good grades?"

"Yes, they are all right."

"How are your English lessons?"

"Good."

"Let me hear you speak English. Say something to that foreign lady at our table."

"Oh no, Dad."

"Come on. I want to hear you talk."

I didn't reveal the fact that I understood everything they said. The son squirmed, then looked at me and said, "How are you?" I replied that I was "Fine, thank you." His father wanted to know what I had said. He told his son to ask me some more questions.

"Do you like it in Japan?"

"Yes, I like Japan very much."

He translated this to his father who told him to ask me what I like about Japan.

"Oh, I like the people, the customs, the food. I like the Kabuki theater."

This was translated to his father who was amazed. "She likes Kabuki? Has she been to a Kabuki show?"

The son asked me those questions and I answered, "Yes, I've been to two shows, and I'm going to another one this afternoon."

The father wanted to see my ticket, so I showed it to them. The son said, "My father says that isn't a very good seat. It is very far in the back."

"I know, but that's all I could spend this time."

By then, it was time to go, so we said our good-byes and bowed to each other. I found my seat in the balcony and I saw the father and son in the choice seats in the front. Shortly before the lights dimmed, the son appeared at my side. He explained that his father had been called away on business and asked if I would like to take his father's seat. I accepted and enjoyed being up close to all the action.

During the intermission, I stood up for a few moments and looked up at the balcony. There, in my seat way in the back, sat the father. He had discretely invented the story that he was called away on business so that I wouldn't feel obligated. I shall never forget his kindness.

37

The New Kimono

NEW YEAR'S DAY is the most important day in Japan. In fact, the whole week is filled with activities, social events, special meals, and dance recitals. The houses are thoroughly cleaned and new mats are placed on the floors. Most important of all, everyone gets a new *kimono* to wear to the festivities.

This was our last New Year celebration in Japan. In June, we would be headed back to the United States. My dance teacher, Yoshiko, was having an extra special show during the New Year week and asked if I was going to buy a new *kimono* for the occasion. She said she could take me to a nice place to look for one.

We set a date and Yoshiko made the arrangements. We arrived at a large house that was far from the small downtown area. A beautifully dressed lady ushered us in and took us to a spacious room where she instructed a young woman to serve us tea. As we kneeled on the large *zabuton* cushions, drinking tea, beautiful models came into the room, one by one, dressed exquisitely in silk *kimono* and embroidered *obi* (wide sash at the waist).

Yoshiko told me to indicate any that I was interested in, and they would come back later for me to review. Each *kimono* was more beautiful than the last one. Finally, I made a decision. Yoshiko helped me choose the proper *obi* to compliment the *kimono* I liked.

The owner had the *kimono* and *obi* folded carefully and placed it in a large silk *furoshiki*.

She told me to take it home, look at it, and if I still wanted it, I could pay her the next day.

Home I went, happy with my decision. When I arrived home, Chiyo was waiting to see what I had chosen. "You buy *kimono*?" she asked.

"No. Not yet. I show to Papa-san first," I answered.

Chiyo wanted to see what I had brought home, so we opened the *furoshiki*. Chiyo caught her breath. "Nice *kimono*! Oh, pretty *kimono*." Then she assumed her protective nature and asked, "How much?" a suspicious look on her face.

I told her how much and she was surprised. "Good price!" She looked at the workmanship in the kimono with approval. Suddenly, she said, "*Hayaku*!" Hurry.

"What?" I asked. "*Hayaku*, make good supper. Make meat, potatoes, good cake, pie. I help."

"Why?" I asked. She said, "Make fine supper for Papa-san. Then show *kimono*. He feel good. He say, 'Okay, you buy.'"

Chiyo rushed around setting the table, peeling potatoes, cutting vegetables. I said, "Chiyo, it's way past five o'clock. Go home." The potatoes were boiling, a meat loaf was in the oven. Chiyo put candles on the table and stood surveying the scene. "Go home, Chiyo. I have this under control."

She said, "Okay. You talk Papa-san tonight?"

I said, "Yes."

She took a deep breath, then said, "Papa-san say no, *I* talk Papa-san." With one more look around, she put on her coat and boots and left.

Byron came home and said, "Candles? What's the occasion?"

I told him I picked out a new *kimono* and Chiyo thought I had to ask Papa-san for permission to buy it. "Chiyo said that if you said I couldn't buy it, *she* was going to speak to you."

"Chiyo's going to speak to me? Little Chiyo who irons my socks and underwear and treats me like the king of this castle?" Byron was shocked with disbelief.

"Fold it up and put it back in that cloth. I want to hear what Chiyo is going to say to me."

The next morning, Chiyo stuck her head in the front door, a happy expectant look on her face. "Papa-san say yes?"

I made a sad face and said, "I didn't ask him. I waited for you to help me."

"*Hayaku!* Make big breakfast, make bacon, eggs." It was Saturday morning and Byron was home. Chiyo pulled out the frying pan and set it on the stove with a look that said "Get busy and cook!"

Breakfast finished, Byron sitting in the living room, I carried the bundle containing the *kimono* into the room. Chiyo followed a few steps in back of me. This was an unrehearsed performance, but we both wanted to hear what Chiyo would say to Papa-san.

"What do you have there?" asked Byron

"A new *kimono*. I wanted you to look at it."

"A *kimono*? How many *kimonos* do you need? You have *kimonos*!"

"But this is a New Year *kimono*. I'm going to dance in a special performance. My other *kimonos* are cotton. This is silk."

Chiyo interjected, smiling, "New Year *kimono*. Everybody have new *kimono* for New Year."

"Well, we're going back to the States in six months. You won't need any *kimono* there."

Chiyo said, "Good *kimono*. Not much money," still smiling and nodding her head.

"How much?" Byron said, trying to look stern.

I told him how much. He said, "Alice, do you realize that kimono costs as much as Chiyo makes in a month?"

There was a long silence. Nobody spoke. Chiyo sat down in an armchair, folded her arms, and looked at the floor. Then Chiyo spoke quietly to Papa-san.

"Okay. My next month. No pay. Okusan *kimono* have."

Tears welled up in Byron's eyes, and he rose quickly and retreated to our bedroom. I followed him as tears were running down my cheeks. We held each other and cried.

"Chiyo surely spoke to Papa-san," said Byron.

We felt ashamed for our pretense and even more remorseful that Chiyo had offered such love and sacrifice. Byron found Chiyo in the kitchen cleaning the breakfast dishes and assured her that Okusan could have the *kimono* and Chiyo would not be giving up her pay.

When the redness left my eyes, I thanked Chiyo for backing me up, and we were both happy about the new kimono.

New Year dance in new kimono

Chiyo and her daughters

38

Sayonara

AND NOW IT was our turn. The day we had eagerly looked forward to during our first year in Japan was fast approaching. Now, four years later, we approached it with mixed feelings: our return to the United States.

When we arrived in this land, our oldest child was ten years old. Barbara was a two-year-old baby. Now, our two oldest children were teenagers. Barbara was ready to start first grade.

Four years ago, I couldn't understand or speak a word of Japanese. Now I was having long conversations and joking with Japanese friends.

When we debarked from the ship in Yokohama, I looked around and thought, *Everyone looks alike—black hair, brown eyes, same height. How do they tell each other apart?*

Now, as my friend, Yoshiko, and I shared our last lunch together, I was describing to her one of my American friends. "Yoshiko, you remember Mary?" Yoshiko shook her head no. "Well, she's tall and thin, has blue eyes, red hair, and freckles." Yoshiko said, "No, Okusan. All Americans look alike to me."

Every month the officer's club had a Sayonara party for the couples who were returning to the States. Byron and I had gone to forty-seven

Sayonara parties. Now, on a Saturday night in May 1962, we joined ten other couples to be feted and honored and sent on our way.

Speeches were made. Toasts were announced. Embarrassing memories were recalled to the amusement of everyone.

Our Japanese dance bandleader, Tiny, took his place in front of the band. As Byron led me to the dance floor, Tiny turned, smiled, and bowed to me, then led the band in a rousing rendition of Glenn Miller's "In the Mood." It was the music I had danced to while wearing a sailor suit four years ago when the officers' wives put on a show. Tiny was the bandleader then. Imagine! He had remembered me from my first year!

Byron hadn't received his orders yet, but we knew we would be leaving in June. Where had the years gone? I knew our chances of seeing our air force friends again were good.

The people in Byron's command usually ended up in San Antonio, Texas. That's where we were scheduled to go.

But what about my Japanese friends? What were my chances of ever seeing them again?

I thought of all the little things that were in my heart, never to be forgotten:

The fragrance of charcoal fires starting up in all the hibachis in town at 5:00 p.m., ready to cook the evening meal.

Japanese music coming from the town's loudspeaker for everyone to enjoy.

The 8:00 a.m. procession of workers coming in from the main gate, walking or bicycling to their various places of employment. All alert, wide awake, content, and pleasant. Housemaids, cooks, clerks, office workers.

School children in uniforms, walking home from school in groups. All happy and talking.

The click-clack sound of wooden *geta* (shoes) on the streets as people walked. Mothers carrying bright-eyed, rosy-cheeked babies on their backs.

The open shops in town and the shopkeepers waving and saying, "*Konichi-wa*" (good day).

Sitting on my back steps on summer mornings, drinking coffee, and watching little girls on the other side of the fence gather wildflowers.

The sound of large drums (*matsuri-daiko*) being beaten on summer nights as the men practice for an upcoming festival.

Dance lessons with Yoshiko. Rest breaks with green tea. Exchanging our philosophies.

Kneeling on a *zabuton* cushion facing Sensei, going through the routine *samisen* exercises.

Chiyo's cheery "*Ohayo gozaimasu*" (good morning) as she comes in the house, takes off her shoes, puts an apron on.

Chiyo's quiet presence during the day, taking care of all of us, humming her "school sayonara" song. Chiyo, you are in my heart forever.

April 1962, Japan

39

Sandwich, Butter, Peanut, Jell-O

BYRON'S NEW ASSIGNMENT in June 1962 was for Kelly Air Force Base in San Antonio, Texas. That was headquarters for Security Service. Many of our friends would be there.

Our return to the United States was not as we had anticipated. A few weeks before we were due to leave Japan, Byron attended a meeting in Tokyo. While he was there, he suffered a heart attack and was taken to a hospital on that base.

I was informed by phone and told not to come to Tokyo. The doctor said they would keep Byron there for an unspecified period of time and then he would be air-evacuated directly to a hospital in the United States.

Byron asked me to stay on base with the children and pack our belongings, call the movers, and drive our car to Hachinohe to have it shipped to San Francisco. I had to get new passports for the children and me, arrange to leave by train, and schedule a flight from Tokyo to the United States on a military troop plane.

Chiyo was a tremendous help in keeping the household running smoothly while I ran around getting all the arrangements made. Friends came by with casseroles and others invited us for meals at their houses, which helped greatly.

Moving day came and Chiyo arrived early with bags of Japanese rice. She also had soy sauce, dried seaweed, and spices that she knew I probably couldn't buy in the States. She planned to smuggle these treasures in the boxes with our household goods.

Japanese men were in every room, putting clothing and books in boxes, carefully wrapping our dishes and knickknacks, and placing them in sturdy barrels. Chiyo stood nearby, deftly hiding bags of rice here and there in the barrels every time the packer turned his back to get more wrapping paper. The packer was wise to her and extricated the contraband each time. He was sympathetic to me, but customs would not permit the food products to enter the United States, and he was not going to lose his job because of a crafty housemaid's tricks.

In the long run, the winner was Chiyo. When we uncrated our washing machine and dryer a month later, there were the bags of rice in the drums of the machines.

Our final day arrived. I decided to walk into town to visit the family-owned shops that Byron had frequented: camera shop, magazine stand, electronics shop, novelty shops, etc. He usually brought little Barbara with him, so I took her with me so they would know who I was saying good-bye for.

As I went to each shop, I explained that my husband had had a heart attack in Tokyo so he couldn't be here to say good-bye. I was saying good-bye for him. They were all concerned and thanked me. They asked when we were leaving, and I told them we were taking the 7:00 p.m. train.

When the children and I arrived at the train station, there was a huge crowd waiting to see us off. There were many American friends, of course. But they were overshadowed by the mass of Japanese people waiting to say good-bye. There was Chiyo and her entire family. Mitsuso and Buz huddled together for a last conversation. Yoshiko, my dance teacher and dearest friend, was there with her mother. Sensei, my *samisen* teacher, the flower-arranging teacher, all the families from Papa-san's favorite stores were there with gifts for us and Papa-san. Even Tiny, the bandleader from the officer's club who had played the jitterbug and cancan music for our show four years ago—even he was there.

After many hugs, bows, and handshakes, the train whistle blew and we had to get on the train. Chiyo broke down and cried out to Patty, Buz, and Kenny. She was saying something about "sandwich butter peanut Jell-O." (She never could get the sequence straight.) I think she was saying she would miss making those sandwiches for the children's lunches.

The train lurched and started to roll. Chiyo ran next to it calling, "Barbara-chan!" Barbara suddenly sensed this was a critical moment and she wailed, "Chiyo!" arms outstretched. Chiyo was still running when I closed my eyes and turned my head. I had lost one mother. Now I was losing another.

40

Letters from Japan

THE FOLLOWING ARE excerpts from letters written by me in Japan to my father and sister in Park Ridge, Illinois. My sister kept the letters and gave them to me when we returned to the United States.

Friday, July 18, 1958

Dear folks,

We're in our new home. Arrived here at 7:30 this morning. We're in the midst of unpacking tonight, but I wanted to stop and write my first impressions of Japan before I got too tired.

We arrived at Yokohama yesterday morning. There was a band on the dock playing "Hi, Neighbor" and other welcoming songs. We rode an army bus to a hotel in Tokyo. It was during that bus ride that I fully realized we were in a foreign country.

There are thousands of little houses everywhere you look, all crowded close together. They're small and look so fragile. They have sliding doors and partitions. The stores are little open markets with half their wares on the sidewalks. All the little stores have bright banners hanging down with Japanese writing on them. The streets are crowded with tiny cars, motor scooters, and bicycles, all going fast.

Many of the people wear our type of clothing, but there are a great many who still wear kimonos and wooden shoes, especially the women. The Japanese women have the sweetest faces! Their complexions are beautiful and their voices are so soft and musical.

We had lunch at the hotel and this is what I got for sixty cents: steak, french fries, corn, rolls and butter, and coffee. Also got a banana split for ten cents extra!

After lunch, we took a taxi and drove around the emperor's palace, then went to the Ginza, which is the shopping center of Tokyo. All the modern department stores are there. They were built after the war. I was amazed at the beautiful things they have for unbelievable prices. They have Noritake china coffee sets: six cups, saucers, plates, sugar and creamer, and coffeepot for $3.

We had to take two taxis from the hotel to the railroad station because of all our luggage. The berths on the train were all made up for the night, and the porter gave us cotton kimonos to sleep in and disposable slippers. The kimonos smelled of soap and disinfectant. Byron unbuttoned his shirt, and the porter helped him to undress. Byron has traveled on Japanese trains before so he knew what to expect. I crept into my berth, pulled the curtain closed, and managed to undress in private, although it was a struggle.

August 27, 1958

We must have arrived here in the midst of the rainy season as I can't remember more than about seven days of sunshine in the six weeks we've been here. If this letter sounds like I'm in a "rainy day" mood, it's because I *am*. I'm so tired of rain and this is supposed to last a few more months. Nothing works right. Salt won't pour, drawers won't open, doors won't close, all our woolens are getting mildew and have to be brushed every day. We have to keep the lights in our closets on all the time to keep mold from forming.

I want to tell you about our housemaid. Her name is Chiyo, and she has already become a very dear part of this family. She speaks only about ten words of English, but we don't find that a barrier. We understand each other quite well. I asked her how many children she has. She said, "Taksan baby-sans," which means "plenty." She has seven children. Her oldest boy is thirty and works as a cook in the Officer's Club. Two of her daughters are in their twenties and are housemaids on the base.

Her youngest boy is ten and is crazy about baseball. Buzzie and Kenny want to meet him, so I'm going to arrange to get him on the base some day. I asked Kenny how they would talk to the boy as he can't understand English and Kenny can't speak Japanese. He said, "We'll write notes to each other."

Chiyo is slowly learning a few more words as Barbara learns them. However, Barbara has started calling flies "horses," and though I've tried to correct her, she still says, "horsey" every time she sees a fly. Today I saw Chiyo with a fly swatter saying "horsey" and pointing to a fly she was going to hit.

She lives in a little Japanese house with her husband and seven children. They have no chairs or beds. They kneel on cushions and eat at a low table. At night, they roll out mattresses to sleep on and they put them away in the morning. For breakfast, they have rice, tea, and a pickle. For lunch, a rice cake or cold cooked rice pressed into a shape like a hamburger, sometimes covered with sesame seeds. For supper, rice, raw fish, soup, and pickle. Japanese babies do not drink milk. They drink rice water. When they are Barbara's age, they eat with chopsticks like an expert.

She has no refrigerator, washing machine, or stove. She cooks over a little pot filled with charcoal. This also provides the heat for the house during the winter months. They have no bathtub. All the town people go to a public bath in town. This is the highlight of the day when friends gather and talk while they bathe in a large community tub. It is a social hour.

She wears a kimono at home. They take their shoes off before they go in the house. When she is in my house, she wears a blouse and skirt. She has become so dear to me.

She adores Barbara and talks and sings to her constantly. Barbara returns her love, and it's so interesting to hear them talk together. Chiyo sings her a Japanese lullaby every afternoon when she puts her down for a nap.

I asked Chiyo if she would bring me some Japanese tea, so she brought a little package of it and a tiny brass teapot. She made a little ceremony of serving it to me. When she poured it out, it just looked like hot water with a little greenish tint. It tasted delicious unlike any tea I've ever had. I can see why she was so proud of it.

Buzzie and Kenny are taking judo lessons from a Japanese teacher. The judo uniform is like a short quilted kimono with white pants. Buzzie wanted me to come and see him throw his teacher up in the air, so I trotted off to the gym one afternoon to see this great feat. After watching the lesson, I came to the conclusion that judo is a sport that requires skill and agility. Much of their lesson consisted of how to fall without breaking their necks.

Then came the moment to watch Buzzie throw his teacher up in the air. Buzzie reached out to grab him but missed, and his teacher sailed up through the air anyway. Buzzie was a little disillusioned when he discovered that it wasn't all his strength that lifted the man over his shoulder.

I have visited the judo lessons several times since then. Sensei (which means "teacher") is a Japanese man about fifty years old. He looks like he doesn't have a neck as his head seems to come right out of his back and shoulders. He doesn't speak one word of English, but the boys seem to understand him. He gives them orders in Japanese.

The boys sit in a row on their knees, wearing their white judo outfits. The lessons begin with the boys bowing to the Sensei and Sensei bowing to them. After a series of exercises, Sensei takes one boy at a time to wrestle with.

The other boys are supposed to be kneeling quietly, waiting their turn, but they get restless and start talking, pushing each other around, and wrestling on the floor. Sensei gets exasperated. Since he doesn't speak English, he lets out a great roar like an animal. The boys stop and look at him with interest and then go right back to their wrestling.

Kenny came home excited the other day after judo lessons. "Mommy, Sensei can speak English now!"

I asked, "What did he say?"

"He said, 'Shut up!'"

The children have an advantage they didn't have while we were living in New York State. They can walk to any place on the base and take part in all the activities that are open to them. The library is only a two-minute walk from home, and they have taken advantage of it since we've been here. They spend their evenings reading, which is better for them than watching television all the time. They can walk to the youth center, the hobby shop, the baseball field, the gym, and the swimming pool. When they go to school, they can come home for lunch as the school is only two blocks away.

I have noticed a marked increase in the children's imaginations and initiative since we are without television. Some days they practice shows in their room and put on some good entertainment for us at night. They rig up a curtain and announce the acts.

September 9, 1958

We took a bus to the town of Hachinohe last Saturday to pick up our car, which had arrived on a small transport ship. Hachinohe is a seaport about twenty-five miles from here. We did a little shopping in the town. I bought some material to make a kimono. I needed an obi to go with it. An obi is a wide belt that you wear with a kimono. The storekeeper took off his shoes and stood on a platform that was covered with straw mats. He motioned for me to sit down on the platform. Then he brought out a great array of obis. I liked the bright colored ones, yellow and red, but he shook his head and pointed to the darker ones. Finally, he pointed to the yellow obi and, with his finger, wrote the number 18 on his palm. Then he pointed to the darker ones and said, "Okusan" (which means wife). He was trying to explain that the bright ones are for young girls.

The trip home in the car was bumpy. It was a narrow country road with a lot of holes. We passed rice fields where men and women were working. They seemed to be enjoying their labor, singing and smiling. They waved to us as we bounced by. The houses we passed were very much alike. They were small unpainted buildings surrounded by a picturesque but rickety-looking fence. The fences are made of twigs tied together. There is a large well near each house where people draw up water in wooden buckets. Each house also had two small outbuildings. One was a bath house. The other was probably an outhouse. There were laundered kimonos hanging out to dry. They don't use clotheslines. Instead, long bamboo poles were inserted through the kimono sleeves and the colorful kimonos seemed to dance in the breeze.

Our air force base had its annual fall festival last week. It's similar to our small town carnivals except there weren't as many exciting rides. They did a good job of improvising though. They had a crude carousel, pony rides, and a "choo-choo-train" driven by a jeep camouflaged to look like a locomotive. They had popcorn stands, rifle shooting, miniature golf, and many booths to try your luck for prizes.

The carnival is set up right inside the main gate and the Japanese people are invited to enjoy the festivities. Raffle tickets were sold for a new MG sports car. A Japanese man won it.

Buzzie was anxious to meet Chiyo's son and we kept looking for them. He came with his older sister and we found them at last. I was really surprised. We expected to see a small-boned, short, little ten-year-old, but he was a strong, husky boy, much taller than Buzzie. When Byron shook hands with him, he bowed his head slightly.

Byron gave Buzzie a dollar's worth of change and told him to take Mitsuso around and treat him to the games. They went off together, Buzzie talking and motioning with his hands. Later, I saw them trying to knock milk bottles down by throwing baseballs. They were both laughing and talking. They came back to us when their money was spent, smiling and eating popcorn that Mitsuso had bought Buzzie. I asked Buzzie later how they could understand each other, and he just shrugged and said, "We just do, that's all. He's real nice and he likes me too."

Sometimes, I think this world would be better off if we could send children as ambassadors to other countries.

September 14, 1958, Sunday

Well, Buzzie has had a busy day today. I'd give my right arm if I could be his age and have the opportunities offered to me that he has. Our housemaid, Chiyo, invited Buzzie to her house today to play with her son who is Buzzie's age.

Chiyo's daughter came to get Buzzie at one o'clock. Buzzie had been counting the minutes after Sunday school, waiting for the time to go to Chiyo's house. I couldn't wait for him to come home and tell me all about it. Buzzie loves to talk, so it's not hard to pump all the details of the visit out of him. He said the whole family was waiting for him at the gate to the base. Even Chiyo's married daughter was there with her little baby strapped on her back.

They walked and walked, zigzagging across fields and footpaths. She lives quite far away from the business section of Misawa. When they got to the house, Buzzie took his shoes off without being told. Their house is small. It has two rooms. The floor is covered with straw mats and the door entering the house is a glass sliding door. Mitsuso showed Buzzie his goldfish and Japanese comic books. The oldest son was sitting at a table, eating rice with chopsticks.

The house was very clean and neat. There were no beds or furniture except the low table and a bookcase with books and the goldfish bowl on it. Mitsuso had made a beautiful big airplane for Buzzie and presented it to him. He must have taken great pains with it as it is one of those made of balsa wood covered with thin red-and-white rice paper. It has a rubber band "motor" and is about two feet long.

Buz brought a bag of Hershey candy bars with him and everyone thanked him. The teenage boy especially liked the chocolate candy.

Mitsuso and Buzzie went outdoors to play baseball. The teenage boy pitched to them. Mitsuso batted the ball so hard it bounced on the roof of the house next door. A man came out of the house and yelled at Mitsuso. Mitsuso was afraid to go in their yard and get the ball, so Buzzie squeezed through the fence and retrieved it.

They flew the airplane for a while until the rubber band broke. Chiyo gave Mitsuso 10 yen, and he motioned for Buzzie to sit on the back of his bike. Off they went to the local store for a new rubber band. Mitsuso kept talking to him in Japanese, asking him questions as they rode on the bike. Buzzie just kept saying, "Yeah."

When they got back, they laid down by the well in the backyard to rest for a while. Then Mitsuso said, "Buzzie," and rambled on in Japanese. Buzzie said, "Okay," and they started to play baseball again. I asked him how he knew what Mitsuso said. He said, "Well, I don't know, but we both felt like playing baseball."

The whole family walked him back to the gate. Chiyo carried the little baby on her back this time. The daughter took Buzzie through the gate and back to our house.

September 20, 1958

Dear folks,

Last night, we went to a *sukiyaki* party. *Sukiyaki* is a delicious Japanese type of beef stew. It has beef, onions, bamboo shoots, noodles, mushrooms, and bean curd, all cooked together in a skillet over a *hibachi* (a small clay pot with charcoal in it).

Everyone had to dress Japanese style and Byron and I won the prize for the best costumes. Chiyo made my *kimono*, a beautiful red silk one, and I had a Japanese style wig made for me in town. Byron had a man's Japanese wig and Chiyo went into hysterics when he put it on. He wore a short *kimono* (called a hoppi coat) and a tea picker's hat, which is made out of straw.

Chiyo and her daughter, Terry, helped us get ready for the party. They wrapped a sash around Byron's waist. They wrapped me up with an *obi*, a wide stiff sash. Now I understand why Japanese women sit so straight. You can't bend with an *obi* on.

At the party, we had to take our shoes off and kneel on cushions at low tables. That's a difficult position to sit in for a whole meal. My feet fell asleep. On each little table, there was a *hibachi* filled with charcoal with *sukiyaki* cooking on it, chopsticks, and a bowl of rice for each person. Chiyo had taught me beforehand how to eat with chopsticks. Japanese girls waited on us, always serving the men first.

There were three beautiful Japanese women to entertain us. They played The *samisen* (a long three-stringed guitar-like instrument) and danced and played games. One of the games was a Japanese version of "rock-paper-scissors."

Many have written asking what our house is like, so I'll try to describe it. It was built by Japanese and has the features of both East and West. It's very small, but adequate for temporary living. We expect to move into a large government house within a few months. These little houses were built to accommodate families who wanted to come over together instead of waiting until their husbands got government housing.

The house is ranch style and has low ceilings. Byron just clears the doorways by one inch and he is five feet, ten inches tall. We have sliding doors for all our closets and "American" doors for entrance to the house. We have three small bedrooms. There is just enough room for twin beds and a bureau in the children's rooms, and a double bed, bureau, and desk in our room. The rest of the house is a combination living room, dining room, and kitchen. The bathtub and sink are made out of tiny little tiles. We are fortunate to have a bathtub that is smooth, well-constructed, and leak-proof. Most of the other bathtubs have tiles slanting in all different directions with corners of the tiles pointing up. They would be very uncomfortable to sit in.

The other day, Buzzie took his football outside to kick it around. Suddenly, I heard all kinds of shouting and commotion. I ran outside to see what happened. About twenty-five Japanese men, who had been painting the house next door, were in the middle of the street with Buzzie, trying to play football. They were having a grand time. Not one of them knew how to hold a football or kick one, but they were running, falling down, and laughing. I don't know why, but wherever you see Buzzie, you see Japanese people.

I had my first den meeting of Cub Scouts last week. (Yes, I got roped into it again.)

One of the little Cubs, a precocious youngster, looked around at his fellow Cubs and remarked, "Well, our den has a lot of rank in it!"

I asked, "What do you mean?"

He said, "Most of us are bears and lions. There's only one bobcat in the whole bunch!"

September 29, 1958

Dear folks,

The typhoon has come and gone, and we're still here, safe and sound. For two days, we looked out the window and watched garbage cans, fences, bushes, etc., flying around outside. Our roof sprung so many leaks we had to use every pot we had. We couldn't use them for cooking anyway as we had no electricity.

Everything has returned to normal now, and we've had sunshine for the first time in four weeks. Hundreds of Japanese men are fixing roofs and mending fences.

An officer and his wife arrived here last week. Yesterday, I took the wife to town to shop for things she needed to set up housekeeping. The wonderful thing about shopping in town is that you can go in with a dollar's worth of yen and come home with your arms loaded.

We arrived in town early in the morning. The Japanese housewives hang their "beds" out the windows to air. They're called futons and are thick padded mattresses. Every house had many colorful futons hanging out the windows.

We went into basket shops where all shapes and sizes of baskets imaginable are lying around every which way. The shopkeepers try so hard to please us. Many times, they give me a small gift when I make a purchase—a handkerchief or a book for my baby-san.

In one store, we saw a young Japanese couple with a beautiful German shepherd dog. He looked just like our dog, King. I went over to them to admire the dog and they smiled. I stooped down and held out my hand to the dog and said, "Shake hands?" The dog looked up at his master questioningly, and his master said something in Japanese to the dog. The dog looked back at me and held up his paw to shake hands.

October 9, 1958

We had some Japanese visitors at our house Friday night. I invited Chiyo's two boys, ages ten and seventeen, and her daughter, Terry. Terry's real name is Teruko. She is in her mid-twenties and works as a housemaid on the base. She speaks English well.

Mitsuso, the ten-year-old, was all dressed up in a new school uniform in honor of the occasion. This was the first time the two boys had ever seen an American-style house.

Their eyes grew big as they looked around. Buzzie took them in his room and showed them his erector set, telescope, etc. They enjoyed looking through his books about weather, atoms, rockets, etc.

Then I showed them our movies of our home in Newburgh, our families, our dog, and the Cub Scouts. We also showed them movies of our family last Christmas: the children hanging up their stockings and trimming the Christmas tree. After the movies, we had chocolate cake and ice cream. This was Mitsuso's first experience at sitting on a chair at a table, eating with a fork. He did very well. He dropped the fork a few times, but soon got the hang of it. (Faster than I learned to eat with chopsticks.)

The older boy thought Barbara was so cute and held her on his lap much of the time. He was especially interested in Byron's shortwave radios and code key. He had just studied code for a year at school.

While the boys were busy in the boys' bedroom trying on cowboy hats and looking at books, Chiyo, Terry and I exchanged comparisons of East and West. We talked about things that women the world over talk about.

I asked Terry if Japanese girls still have to marry a man whom her family chooses for her. She said it is different now, especially in Misawa where they see so many Americans. Some Japanese girls marry GIs. Some girls marry Japanese men of their own choice, but most girls follow the old system of family arranged marriages.

This is how a marriage is arranged. When a family has a son of marriageable age, they ask a friend (the go-between) to find a suitable wife for him. She scouts around the town and nearby villages for likely candidates. She brings back pictures of five or six girls and their parents. She has also left pictures of the son and his parents for the girls' families to look at.

The son usually leaves the choice up to his family as he relies on their wisdom and experience. When a girl is chosen, a secret meeting is arranged between the young couple and both families. This usually takes place in a dim restaurant or a movie theater. Friends and neighbors must not know of this meeting in case one of the families decides against the marriage. This is to save face. During the "accidental meeting," the families look each other over and make up their minds. The young couple sits far apart from each other. Terry says most Japanese girls are too shy to look up.

After the meeting, if both families approve, the wedding date is set and the marriage takes place. The bride's name is taken off her family's register in the town's records and written on her husband's family register. She goes to live with her husband's family where the mother-in-law is the boss. If the bride is lazy or does not please her mother-in-law, she could be sent back to her family, divorced. This would be a terrible disgrace.

Chiyo said her parents arranged her marriage when she was only one year old. Both families knew each other well.

A Japanese baby is spoiled (by our standards) until it is six years old. They are never spanked. The babies are carried on Mama's back everywhere she goes. When big sister comes home from school, she takes her turn at carrying the baby. The children eat whenever they are hungry, sleep when they feel like it, and are allowed all the freedom they want.

I asked Terry how they could have control over their children under such a system. The Japanese children I've seen are always well-mannered, quiet, never crying. She said that comes from the fear of being ridiculed. They learn correct manners by example of the family. There is no other way to act except modest and polite. They learn to bow from the time they are able to stand. If they make a mistake in manners, they are afraid they would be laughed at. The children are shy. That is why they don't make noise in public.

When they start school, they are told they represent the family now, and they wouldn't dare make a mistake to disgrace their home. Little girls are taught early to respect men. They must never walk on the section of the floor that their father or older brothers sleep on.

When Father comes home from work, Mother drops everything and brings him a basin of hot water and a towel to wash his hands. Then she gets supper on the table quickly. I said we do the same thing in America, but our husbands find their own hot water to wash their hands with.

Chiyo was curious to know if I had my babies in a hospital and if a man doctor helped me. I said yes to both questions and explained there is a law that a doctor should be present when the baby is born if possible. Chiyo never heard of such a thing. A Japanese woman would never think of having a man doctor. An old woman with much experience comes to help them in their home.

Chiyo said, with much pride, "Japanese mothers nurse their babies." I said, "American mothers do too." She was surprised at this. She thought all American babies were brought up on a bottle.

She said, "Japanese women do not cry out in childbirth." I said, "There are many different kinds of people in America. Some cry out and some don't." I went on to relate the amusing experience I had when Barbara was born. My husband had been allowed to stay by my bed in the labor room. As the labor contractions became closer and more intense, I tried hard not to make any noise because he was there and I wanted to be brave. At the moment the baby was being born, Byron said to me, "I've got a pain in my back from sitting here so long."

This usually brings amused chuckles from any American woman I tell this to. I waited for the laughter, but there was none. Terry said, "So, of course, you had to massage his back."

I said, "No, I just went ahead and had the baby."

"Poor man!" they said.

November 10, 1958

Just a note to let you know we're still here in case you heard about the earthquake we had. We get small earthquakes all the time here, sometimes three a week. They are hardly noticeable and only last a minute or two. Dishes rattle and the floor shakes a little.

But this was something different. This quake was only 0.25 points less than the great earthquake of 1923 in Japan. I can't tell you what a queer feeling it was. It was about eight o'clock in the morning. Patty was walking across the living room when she tripped over her feet. Then she started to laugh and pointed at the Madam Butterfly doll on the bookshelf. It was doing a dance, the fan waving and the parasol bouncing. Lamps were sliding back and forth and the stove was making an awful racket.

I ran to the door and saw the parked cars outside rolling back and forth. What an odd feeling! Kenny had just started to ride his bike to school when he fell off like he was thrown from a horse. I called him to come in the house.

We all gathered together in the living room and just stood there. Dishes were flying out of the cupboards and crashing to the floor. The floor of the house was moving in a back-and-forth motion like someone was shaking it. Then the whole house felt like it was being picked up and thrown back down. Each time the house came down, there was a loud banging sound. I thought it was the end of the world. From where we stood in the living room, I could see through the window all the Japanese people walking to their places of work. They didn't seem to be concerned about what was going on.

After a while, it was all over. The children went to school and Chiyo came in. I asked her if she knew there had been an earthquake, and she smiled and said, "Hai" and put her apron on and we picked up the broken dishes.

It's really growing cold here and the sky looks like we'll have snow. The stores downtown remain open as they did all summer. The store people have hands that are purple from the cold, but still they smile and bow politely. Some of the stores have little clay pots with a little charcoal burning and a tea kettle over it. Friends and relatives kneel around it and talk.

Our house is only about fifty feet from the high fence that encircles this base and separates it from the town. From my window, I can see Mrs. Yamaguchi wash her *kimonos* in a wooden tub outside and hang them on a bamboo pole to dry. Her baby is strapped to her back all the time, usually asleep. Her other children play around the yard in their bright *kimonos*.

At night, there is a pretty orange-colored glow coming from the side of her house that faces us. That side of her house is all paper sliding doors, and the dim light inside looks so warm and cozy. But I wonder how they keep warm. They are probably all gathered around the *hibachi*.

Kenny has earned his green belt in judo. Buzzie had his tenth birthday yesterday. We gave him a muscle builder. It was one of those springy things you pull apart. He pulled on it for a few minutes and ran into his bedroom. I peeked in and saw him examining his arm to see if there were any muscles yet.

November 20, 1958

Well, the Hula-Hoop craze has hit Misawa Air Base, and everyone is going crazy over them, including the grown-ups. The base exchange has been getting a shipment of fifty hoops every day, and there are thousands of people trying to buy them for their children.

I read that the geishas are doing the Hula-Hoop at geisha parties instead of Japanese dancing. The streets in Tokyo are full of Japanese children with Hula-Hoops.

We had our first real cold day today. It was bitter cold and the wind from the ocean blew right through this little house. Even Chiyo was cold! She came in this morning and stood by our heater, warming her hands, and for the first time, she accepted a cup of coffee to warm her up.

I asked her how it was in her house, and she said it was just as cold inside as it was outside. They sleep on the floor and have just a little charcoal pot to cook and warm the house. They bundle up in padded *kimonos* and put metal hot-water bottles next to them.

One day, while she was ironing, I heard Chiyo singing "Jesus Loves Me" in a sweet voice. This surprised me as I know she is a Buddhist. I asked her daughter, Terry, where her mother had learned that song. She explained that Chiyo had learned it at a mission when she was a little girl and lived in Hirosaki. Chiyo has many pleasant memories of her hometown. It is famous for a large park with cherry blossoms. Her eighty-nine-year-old mother still lives there.

Chiyo has the patience of a saint. I have never seen her upset. She radiates such happiness and love in her daily life. It is not just grim resignation with her lot in life, but a true happiness that carries her through life. We speak to each other all day, but I don't really know how. I knew a few words of Japanese and she knows a few words of English, but we communicate. She's a very intelligent woman and has a keen sense of humor. We find many things to laugh at together.

December 18, 1958

Sorry I haven't had any time to write for a while. We've moved to a nice new apartment. It's clean and warm and we have all the hot water we can use.

I may have remarked once that I never saw Chiyo lose her temper, but I must retract that statement now. These apartments have just been built, and we are the first family to move in. After we had been given the key to the apartment, Chiyo and I came over one day and washed all the floors and waxed them good. They looked beautiful when we finished.

The next day, we brought some dishes and sheets to the apartment and found the door open and fifty Japanese laborers in our apartment having a party. They had cooked coffee on the new stove and were sitting all over the floor with their muddy boots on, smoking and grinding out their cigarettes on the floor.

They had been putting up storm windows all morning for the apartments and apparently thought this was still an empty apartment where they could take a coffee break. They used a pass key.

Well, I never saw Chiyo act so fast! She landed into them with a broom, jabbering in Japanese while the men scattered out the doors. She grabbed two of them and made them wash and wax all the floors. They weren't doing it right to suit her, so she stood right over them, talking all the time. I caught a few of the words she was saying, "Mama-san very mad! Papa-san big *honcho*! You hurry up!"

When they finished waxing, they bowed sheepishly to me, backing out the door. Chiyo looked at me with a big grin on her face, proud of her aggressiveness.

I've been baking cookies for orphanages and for the airmen at isolated places in Japan. Our apartment is also the receiving place for all the donations of candy, cookies, and presents to be packed in boxes for the orphanages and for the airmen. We have a steady stream of wives bringing in gaily wrapped packages. Patty is learning how to make cookies for this project.

Merry Christmas to all of you. We plan to go to the Christmas Eve service at church and have a few friends over later. We will invite a few men over for Christmas dinner (the ones who don't have their families here yet).

December 29, 1958

Well, Christmas is past, but things haven't slowed down around here. The children are still home on vacation and this house has been filled with boys and girls today. They're playing with those telephones you sent them. Patty's girl friends are in her room, giggling and ringing the boys' telephone where all Buzzie's and Kenny's friends are congregated. They can really hear each other on those phones.

The day before Christmas, Chiyo came in with her arms loaded with presents. There was something for each one of us. They were wrapped so pretty and had tags on them with our names written in English. I found out she had asked Patty to write our names for her and she copied them on the tags. The gifts were lovely and reflected much thoughtfulness and sacrifice on her part. She gave me a beautiful lacquer set of dishes with ivory chopsticks.

We loaded Chiyo down with gifts for her whole family on Christmas Eve and drove her partway home. I've never been in her house, although the children have been there many times. I was hoping I would see it this time, but we can't drive all the way there because the street is too narrow and the mud is too thick. She insisted on getting out of the car and carrying the packages by herself.

A few short years ago, we were fighting a long and bitter war with these people, and now we are exchanging Christmas presents with them. Byron was at Pearl Harbor when the attack started, and this year, he was so excited to buy just the right gift (an electric train set) for Chiyo's ten-year-old boy. Chiyo's husband was in the war and now Chiyo sacrifices a large part of her small salary to buy Christmas gifts for us, and her husband smiles and talks nicely to our children whenever they go to her house.

When Japan surrendered, the United States declared that the emperor was not divine. The people of Japan were told the emperor was just a human being and was not descended from the sun god.

It must be hard to erase a life's teachings. The other day, Princess Chichibo of the imperial family made a little speech on the radio at the

Rice Bowl football game. Chiyo came into the living room and made a low bow to the radio.

New Year is the big holiday for the Japanese. They have been busy cleaning their houses and buying gifts. Everyone gets a new *kimono*. They decorate the doors to their houses with bamboo sticks and sprays of pine and go visiting friends and relatives. They celebrate for over a week. All Japanese automatically become a year older on New Year's day.

January 19, 1959

The base has started a training course in survival for the wives. This is a series of lectures and movies about what to do in the event of an atomic war. They tell us the men will be too busy with their duties to worry about taking care of their families. It's up to the wives to handle the safety of the family and to know what to do and where to go.

Every housing area has its designated underground tunnel to go to when the siren goes off. We're supposed to gather up our children, grab our ready kits, and get in the tunnels within one minute. If we can't find all our children within that one minute, we're to forget about them and get in the tunnel.

This must have been thought up by some man who has no wife or children. Can you imagine any mother worrying about her ready kit when she has one minute to find her children? The wives are already figuring out a better solution. We're stashing our ready kits in the tunnels now.

We had a little Japanese visitor here last week for lunch. She was a fourteen-year-old schoolgirl from Aomori. Her class was invited to our base to see how an American school functions and to visit different places on the base. Some of the wives invited the Japanese children to their homes for lunch. Patty invited a girl, and we were all watching out the window for her.

Chiyo had fixed a delicious lunch of fried rice, egg rolls, and tea. When we saw them coming, Chiyo showed me how to open the door and what to say. She told me to open the door and hide myself behind it, just peeking my head out a little to say, "*Ohayo goziamasu. Hai, dozo.*" Good morning, please enter.

I did as Chiyo taught me and the girl said, "How do you do. My name is Keiko Nanga." We all breathed a sigh of relief. The girl could speak English. It was short-lived though as we soon found out it was the *only* English she knew. Apparently, her class learned this short phrase and practiced it for a long time before they arrived at the base.

As I introduced her to Buzzie and Kenny, she said the same thing, bowing politely each time, with a special low bow to Buzzie who is the eldest son. Then she opened her *furoshiki* (a cloth tied in four corners to make a bundle) and took out three beautiful bean bags she had made of colorful silk. She showed Patty how all Japanese girls can juggle them, counting in Japanese. Patty tried, with no success. I had no luck with the bean bags either, but Chiyo did it like a professional. Keiko gave Patty the bean bags as a present. She also gave her a cute little *kokeshi* doll (a friendship doll).

When we sat down to lunch, she used chopsticks and carried on a sweet conversation with Chiyo. I love to hear two Japanese women talk. Their voices are so musical. When they left for school, we gave Keiko a box of chocolate chip cookies and some American comic books.

February 4, 1959

Things go on as usual here. We had two earthquakes last week, but they don't bother us much anymore.

I passed my first aid test, so now I'm fully prepared to bandage my children's skinned knees and "treat for shock." That "treat for shock" was drilled into us for everything from a burned finger to a stubbed toe. My first aid kit looks like a doctor's office. The instructors came around to our houses to check our ready kits and first aid kits.

Patty has started judo lessons and tried on her judo *gi* tonight. The boys are green belts now and are quite proud of their progress. Patty has had just one lesson, so the boys decided to give her a few pointers tonight. As they both came toward her, she grabbed each one of them and sent them sailing across the room. Buzzie is worried that Sensei won't last long with Patty there.

Speaking of throwing people around, the other day I played a dumb trick on Byron. It was payday, and when he came home from work, I stood behind a wall near the door and stuck my arm out, saying, "Gimme all your money!" Unfortunately, I forgot he was trained in guerilla warfare and was prepared for sudden unexpected movements. He automatically grabbed my arm and I went somersaulting into the air, crashing to the floor on my back. Chiyo rushed into the room and stood there, horrified.

When I opened my eyes, Byron was bending over me. He was so worried and apologetic. Then he broke all the rules I had just learned in my first aid course. He wasn't treating me for shock, and he was *moving* me. He pulled me up from under my arms and took me out to the car. We were on our way to the hospital to check for broken bones. Kenny was in the backseat. He said, "Why is Mommy going to the hospital? Is she going to have another baby? Will it be a Japanese baby?" That made me laugh and I could feel pain in my ribs.

While we were waiting to be called into the examining room, Byron looked at me sheepishly and asked, "Are you going to tell the doctor what happened?" Well, I did tell the doctor what happened, and it became part of my medical record, along with Kenny's "dewclop" record.

There were no broken bones and I learned a valuable lesson. Never surprise Byron. His father brought a breakfast tray to Byron right after World War II, thinking he was giving him a treat. He leaned over and gently tapped Byron as he slept. Byron's fist sent the tray and his father across the room.

Barbara is picking up a lot of Japanese words. There are times when I can't understand what she's saying. The other day she was reading a book, talking in a strange language.

Byron asked, "What's she saying?"

"I don't know. Chiyo, is Barbara speaking Japanese?"

Chiyo listened to her and answered, "No Japanese. English?"

I said, "No English."

We listened again. Barbara kept turning the pages of the book and talking.

Chiyo said, "Maybe Korean!" and went back to her work.

March 16, 1959

My family is growing up! I bought Patty her first bra last week. Buzzie is losing a lot of his baby teeth. He keeps his loose teeth in his mouth, hanging by a thread. He said he's learned by experience that it's more profitable to put his tooth under his pillow the day after payday, so he keeps them in his mouth until the strategic time.

Chiyo wanted to know why Buzzie puts his teeth under the pillow and gets money for them. I explained the fairy comes during the night and takes the tooth and leaves money.

She said a mouse (*nezumi*) comes during the night and takes the Japanese children's teeth, but he doesn't leave money.

Chiyo is a wonderful person, but she is afraid of the telephone. If my friends call when I'm not home, she answers saying, "*Okusan* no home. Commissary go," and hangs up before they can leave a message.

I tried several times to call our house. When Chiyo answers with a scared-sounding hello, I say, "Chiyo, this is Alice—" and before I can tell her what I called about, she says, "*Okusan* no home. Commissary go!" and hangs up.

However, when someone comes to the house and I'm not home, her manner is altogether different. She will stand and admire my friend's clothes and go into great detail about where I have gone, supplementing her limited English words with gestures. My neighbor called on me one afternoon while I was at dance rehearsal for the show we're putting together. Chiyo went to the door and said, "No home. Dansu," and she gave a great imitation of the cancan, kicking up her heels in great style as she has seen me practice at home.

April 10, 1959

Dear folks,

For the first time since we arrived here almost a year ago, Byron took several days off. He started the first day of his leave with a bang! We were sitting in the living room having a second cup of coffee about 8:30 that morning, just relaxing. The children had left for school and Chiyo was quietly going about her duties. Byron's eyes wandered to the small hole in our living room wall. There is a little metal disk up near the ceiling with a tiny hole in it. I never paid any attention to it.

Byron said, "You know, ever since we moved into this apartment, I've wondered what that hole is there for." We started guessing what it could be. I offered numerous ideas, but nothing very logical. At last, I said, "Maybe it's the communists listening to every word we say. Maybe they are bugging us." That stimulated Byron's imagination so he got his shortwave radio earphones, stood on a chair, and plugged the wire into the hole.

Well, we were in for a surprise! A loud fire alarm went off all through the building, red lights flashed in our hallway, and people were running from their apartments in their pajamas. The fire alarm made such a deafening roar we couldn't think straight, and while we were trying to call the fire department to tell them there was no fire, we heard two big fire engines come wailing to a stop followed by the fire chief's car.

When the Japanese firemen rushed up our stairs with hoses, Byron opened the door and looked at them with a straight face and asked, "What's the matter?" The men examined the fire alarm box in our hallway and saw that it wasn't broken. Byron said, "No fire here. Must be a short circuit somewhere."

We left the apartment shortly afterward, and as we were walking toward our car, a jeep drove up and two air policemen got out. As they passed us, they asked, "Which building had the fire alarm?" With the innocent face of an angel, Byron replied, "Building 882," pointing to our building, and we continued to our car and drove off.

When we got home, I asked Chiyo if the air policemen came to the apartment. She said, "Yes." I asked her what she said to them. She made an innocent-looking face and said, "I say, 'I dunno, I dunno.'" Byron was so impressed with her loyalty, he raised her salary.

As the day progressed and neighbors started making remarks about children playing with fire alarms, Byron's conscience took over and he went down to the fire chief and confessed. The fire chief said it was okay. His men had a good fire drill. Byron congratulated the fire chief on the efficiency of his men and they parted friends.

May 16, 1959

It's a rainy Saturday night; the children are taking baths and getting ready for bed, so I'll start this letter while it's peaceful.

We went to the city of Hirosaki for the cherry blossom festival a few Sundays ago. It was a long trip by train. We had to leave at 5:00 a.m. The train was beautifully decorated with paper cherry blossoms. When we arrived at Hirosaki, the station was decorated with cherry blossoms, and the cherry blossom song was playing over a loudspeaker.

The park was beautiful and inspiring. The blossoms were in full bloom. The cherry blossom is a national symbol to the Japanese. It has symbolic meaning as the blossom doesn't wither and die on the tree, but floats down to earth in full flower.

People were everywhere. The Japanese were taking pictures of us and we took pictures of them. Many were sitting around straw mats having their lunches. They were in a gay mood. Some of the young girls in colorful *kimonos* were dancing. There were also some men dancing. As we passed, they waved at us and invited us to join them. I joined a few of the groups and watched the dancing and listened to the singing. Byron stood a few feet away and took pictures.

Last week, there was Boys' Day. On Boys' Day, every family puts a pole up on their roof with big fish made out of silk attached to the pole. One fish for every boy in the household. The fish are hollow, something like a windsock at an airfield. When the wind blows, it puffs out the fish, making them look like they're swimming. The fish (carp) stands for strength. The fish fight against the stream to reach their goal.

June 2, 1959

There are a lot of people going back home this month and many new families arriving here. June and July seem to be the big turnover months. We've had Sayonara parties for various friends who are on their way back home.

It's refreshing to see all the newcomers. We can tell they are new because their shoes all fit them and all their accessories match: shoes, handbags, hats. There is such a short supply of shoes and clothes in the base exchange and a poor selection of sizes. I was in the base exchange yesterday, happy because there was a shipment of boys' shirts. A woman, obviously a newcomer, announced, "This is the worst children's department I've ever seen!" The rest of us remembered thinking the same thing the first day we got here.

July 15, 1959

The new general and his wife arrived on the base yesterday. Nobody has met them yet, but Buzzie had lunch at their house today. Leave it to him to find his way in their back door! It seems they have a boy Buzzie's age and they were playing together all morning. The general and his wife were carrying lamps and little odds and ends into their house, so Buzzie pitched in and helped them, so the general invited him to stay for lunch.

Buzzie decided the general's wife was so nice he would let her see his lizard. She reacted the same way I did the first time I saw it and asked Buzzie if he would mind if the lizard waited outside while he was eating lunch.

There will be a formal reception for the general and his wife Friday night when I will meet them for the first time. Buz had the fun of meeting them informally before anyone else did.

August 13, 1959

Last week, we moved into a new house. At last, we are settled for the next three years. We are assigned houses according to the number of children we have, but we had to wait a year before a larger house was available for us. I wish you could see it. It's a mansion!

We have a living room, dining room, kitchen, four and a half bedrooms, two and a half bathrooms, and a laundry room. Byron uses the half bedroom for his shortwave radios and his photography lab. It has a little bathroom next to it that he can use for developing pictures.

Kenny and Buzzie are in Little League now. They are on different teams, and we spend almost every weekday at the baseball fields. We either hurriedly eat a sandwich before the games or we come home and have a very late supper after the games. It's hectic, but we don't want to miss seeing the games.

Patty has joined a softball team. She's the catcher. The other day, she watched me using a deodorant and asked what that was for. I told her it stops perspiration. Yesterday, as she was leaving to play softball, I noticed she had white stuff smeared all over her face. I asked her what that was and she said, "It's your Arrid deodorant. My face gets awful sweaty when I'm playing ball."

She's also going to a charm school this summer at the Youth Center. I don't know what they're teaching her, but she still takes pride in stuffing her mouth with bubble gum and blowing larger bubbles than any of her friends.

Oh, Chiyo's daughter, Terry, has a boyfriend, and it looks pretty serious. He is a Japanese man, works on the base as a cook. Terry says he is bashful. She describes him as a "Nice Japanese man. No drink. No smoke. Very tall, 5'6'." He is thirty-three years old. Terry is twenty-five. She is going to meet his parents next Sunday. She couldn't decide whether she would wear a *kimono* or dress "western style." I loaned her a pretty light-blue dress. It fit her perfectly and she's going to wear that.

November 1, 1959

There is a distinctive aroma in the air at this time of the year that we will probably miss when we're back in the States. At four o'clock, every housewife in town starts her charcoal fire to cook the evening rice. As I look out our back door, I can see blue smoke rising from every little house in town and the smell of the charcoal fires is pleasant on the cold air.

Last night was Halloween and all of us had someplace to go, so Chiyo stayed to babysit with Barbara. This is the first year that trick-or-treat has been allowed on the base. I knew Chiyo would be bewildered by all the kids ringing our doorbell dressed up as witches and devils, etc.

We tried to explain what it was all about. Fortunately, just before we all left, some little boys came to our door, and we were able to show Chiyo that all she had to do was give them some candy.

Byron and I were asked to chaperone the preteen party at the Youth Center that night. It was quite an experience. Patty and Buzzie belong to preteens and I was curious to see how they behaved themselves there. I needn't have worried. Their behavior was prim and straitlaced, but I'm afraid they were ashamed of me.

I don't know what's happening to this younger generation, but I don't think they know how to have fun. From 6:00 p.m. to 9:00 p.m., I never saw one of them laugh or even smile. Most of the dancing was rock and roll. Those kids could dance for hours, chewing their bubble gum, with deadpan expressions on their faces.

I went up to a tall twelve-year-old boy and asked him to show me how to rock and roll. After I got the hang of it, I was having a grand time and Byron was sitting in a corner laughing. Then I saw Patty looking at me as if she wanted to die. I found out later I was dancing with the big wheel of the eighth grade!

Byron and I had never been chaperones before, and we were a little hazy as to what our duties were. Kids that age never stay in the room where the party is held for more than five minutes at a time. There is a steady stream to the bathroom. We were wondering if this was a generation of weak kidneys until we noticed how much lemonade they were consuming.

Byron played some Glenn Miller jitterbug records of the 1943 vintage. All dancing stopped. The kids just sat around with bored expressions. After a while, it was plain to see the kids were getting restless. There were more trips to the bathroom, a bitter lover's quarrel was brewing in the snack bar, and two boys went outside to have a fight. Byron followed them out to stop them, but they both had bloody noses by the time he broke it up.

Patty and her girl friends came to our rescue by informing Daddy that *nobody* dances to that old-fashioned music. They switched to rock and roll and the party was in full swing again.

We got a kick out of Buzzie. All the girls were talking about how cute he is and were hoping he'd ask them to dance. One girl told him a few weeks ago that he looks like Ricky Nelson, and he spends hours every morning combing his hair in Ricky Nelson style, missing the school bus as a result.

Byron and I were reminiscing about our young days and laughing when Patty came up to us with a threatening look and said, "Mommy, please don't laugh so much. Everybody's looking at you!" Obviously, I was breaking the laughing law.

We were glad to leave that stuffed-shirt party and go on to our own party at the Officer's Club where everyone was dressed in silly Halloween costumes, dancing the cha-cha and jitterbug, *laughing,* and having the time of their lives.

41

Watch Out for the Rattlesnakes!

B YRON HAD BEEN sent to a hospital at Lackland Air Force Base in San Antonio, Texas.

The children and I arrived in San Francisco and I picked up our car at the dock. After driving on the left side of the road in Japan for four years, it was difficult to adjust to driving on the right side. San Francisco was not the best place to break the habit.

Some horn-honking and choice words from other drivers helped me break the habit quickly.

Once we got to the desert, it really didn't matter what side of the road we were on. We didn't see a car coming from either direction for miles. That ride from San Francisco to San Antonio, Texas, was unforgettable. Our car wasn't air-conditioned, the children were hot and irritable, we traveled endless miles on a flat surface with nothing to see but sand on all sides of us. There were no rest stops, and I kept falling asleep at the wheel from the heat and monotony. The children yelled, "Mom! You're sleeping!" and I would wake up and aim the car at the watery-looking horizon.

Somehow, we arrived safely in San Antonio and our family was happily reunited. Byron had been released from the hospital and was assigned to headquarters, Security Service at Kelly Air Force Base in San Antonio. We stayed on the base at family guest quarters while we looked for a permanent place to live.

Barbara was watching cartoons on television the morning after we arrived, and she came running to me. "Mommy, Popeye can speak English!" She had watched Japanese TV at Chiyo's house a few times, and although Japan used our cartoons, they dubbed in their own spoken language. The Lucy Show, John Wayne Westerns, and other favorites were also dubbed.

This would be Byron's last assignment. He would be eligible to retire in four years, so we decided to buy a house rather than rent. What better place to retire? There were many military bases in the area. We would have the benefits of military hospitals and doctors free of charge, several large commissaries where groceries were cheaper than supermarkets, and many of our air force friends were retiring in the area.

We found a lovely ranch-style house that had just been built. It was perfect for our family. As soon as we signed all the papers, we moved right in. Our furniture hadn't arrived from Japan yet, but the house had built-in kitchen appliances. Friends loaned us dishes, cooking utensils, and sleeping bags.

The day we brought our suitcases to our new house, friends invited us over for dinner. Dinner conversation became terrifying as our well-meaning hosts warned us about rattlesnakes. They explained that a new housing development like ours had many rattlesnakes on the loose because their nests had all been dug up. They told us tales of people finding rattlesnakes slithering around on their floors because they had left their patio sliding door open. By the time we left their house, my hair was standing on end.

We entered our new house and quickly made a search of all the rooms. After we turned off the lights and settled in our sleeping bags, I was wide awake, waiting for the attack of the snakes.

At midnight, I poked Byron until he was awake. "What's the matter?" he asked.

"I hear a snake!" I hissed.

"What do you mean, you *hear* a snake?"

"I hear it crawling. Get up and turn on the light."

The only light source in the empty room was the ceiling light. To reach the wall switch, Byron had to walk across the room. He obligingly got up and started to walk toward the switch.

"Don't step on the snake," I warned in a whisper.

Light flooded the room and we looked for the phantom snake. We shook out our sleeping bags. Byron made the rounds through the other rooms and returned reporting no sign of snakes. He reached for the wall switch, but I insisted we keep it on.

Eventually, I fell asleep, certain that no rattlesnake would dare come in a room with the light on.

42

Shall We Dance?

OUR HOUSE AT 314 Fantasia Drive was ideal for our family. The community swimming pool and recreation area was less than a block away, and there were various family activities during the week and dances on Saturday nights for the teenagers. Patty was fourteen, Buz was thirteen, Ken was eleven, and Barbara was six years old when we moved in. They spent the summer getting acquainted with the young people in the neighborhood.

I spent the time unpacking our household goods when they arrived from Japan and from storage. The job was enhanced by the discovery of Chiyo's clever hiding places for her contraband rice and soy sauce.

Summer ended and the children started classes in their new schools. Barbara entered first grade. The house was suddenly quiet, giving me time to reflect on the happy, busy days when we lived in Japan. I missed Chiyo and Yoshiko greatly. I remembered the delicious fried rice Chiyo made. I missed hearing her hum songs as she worked. To break the silence of the house, I unpacked my samisen and practiced the music Sensei and I had played together. What would be the use for this music here in Texas? I thought back to the daily dance lessons with Yoshiko: the laughter, the quiet rest times while we drank tea.

What was the use of all those lessons and practice now that I was back in the United States?

Just for the fun of it, I decided to place an ad in the daily newspaper. After all, I had a license to teach dance. Let's see if anyone was interested in Japanese dance lessons. To my surprise, I received many calls. I quickly designated Saturday afternoons for teaching and set up classes according to age. My new students ranged in age from five years old to adults. The younger dancers were girls, but the adults who inquired were men and women from all walks of life. Luckily, I had studied men's dances. Several Japanese ladies who married American servicemen arrived that first Saturday. They had always wanted to learn to dance in Japan, but either their families couldn't afford lessons or World War II was in progress when they were teenagers and lessons were suspended.

Our family room was turned into a dance studio on Saturday afternoons and the classes began. Mothers who brought their young daughters watched proudly as their children followed my instructions. In all, there were about fifteen people who signed up for lessons. I couldn't believe there was such an interest, and I wondered if they would return for more lessons. The next Saturday, they all returned, eager to learn more.

About a month after I put that ad in the newspaper, I received a call from a local television station. The woman who called said she had seen my ad and wanted to follow up on it. She wanted to know if I had any responses to the ad and if I was teaching. I told her I had fifteen students. She asked me how I learned Japanese dancing, so I answered her questions and she showed a genuine interest. She asked if my students and I would dance on TV. I told her the students were not ready yet, but perhaps they could in the future.

She asked if I would perform some dances on her TV show. She wanted to interview me on the show and have me explain the movements in some of the dances. A half-hour program was what she planned. It would be a taped program to be played later in the month. I agreed and went to the studio for the recording. Dressed in a dancing kimono, I performed a variety of dances from folk dancing to classical. The interview went well, and we watched it on TV a few weeks later.

The day after the TV show aired, I started receiving more calls from people wanting to take lessons. I also received calls from various clubs asking our group to perform for some of their special events. I had written to

Yoshiko to ask her to send kimonos, fans, and *tabis* (dancing socks) for my students, and she had sent boxes of costumes, but now I realized I would have to find other ways to outfit my rapidly growing group.

There were five military bases in the San Antonio area. Many Japanese girls had married American servicemen and were living off base. I asked around until I found a Japanese woman who could sew. Her name was Jeannie, a name she had given herself when she got her citizenship papers. She was a warm, friendly person who agreed to sew kimonos for our group.

Jeannie became a valued friend. We talked about many things, including my friends back in Japan and how difficult it was for me to write to them, writing Japanese words with the English alphabet. She offered to teach me how to write in Japanese. She was an excellent teacher and I looked forward to our lessons. She started by teaching me to write in *katakana*, a sort of Japanese alphabet. She assigned a group of characters for me to learn each week, and I could write them and pronounce them by the next week's lesson.

After we finished the basic forty-six characters, we studied the fifty-eight modifications to those characters. Once these were mastered, I could write letters to Yoshiko and to Chiyo's daughter, Terry, in their own phonetic characters. Before that, I was using our alphabet to spell Japanese words. Our alphabet and written words were as foreign to the Japanese as their characters are to us.

The basics sufficed for my purposes, but I became fascinated with the Japanese kanji symbols. There is a symbol for each word and the symbol is actually a picture. When you know what the picture means, you have no problem reading it. The word *tree* actually looks like a tree. The word *forest* is formed by drawing three trees. There are 1,850 essential characters. Some characters take twenty-three strokes to draw. I bought a book that has all 1,850 characters and how to write them. The strokes are made in a prescribed order. I still like to study those symbols and marvel at how those drawings evolved into words.

When I came to Jeannie's house for my writing lessons, she would invite me to stay for lunch. It was always a Japanese-style meal, and soon, she was teaching me how to cook my favorite meals. I have a notebook filled with her recipes, one of which came in handy years later in another chapter.

Saturday lessons continued, and each class became a family to me and to each other. The enthusiasm the students presented was an inspiration to me and I looked forward to the lessons each week.

With Jeannie's help making kimonos for the dancers and Yoshiko sending fans and *tabis,* our dancers were making great progress. The kimono sleeves are used in some dances to express emotions such as shyness or sadness (hiding one's face behind a sleeve). The fans were essential to portray many things, leaves falling, butterflies (using two fans), and samurai swords (a closed fan).

Patty, who had never displayed an interest in Japanese dancing, decided to join our group. Even little Barbara wanted to be a part of the children's class. Both of them progressed quickly because they had the advantage of watching me dance in Japan. Within six months, we were putting on shows that were well received and that generated more invitations to perform.

Other television stations invited us to dance. On one of the TV shows, I played the *samisen* while my class of five-year-old children sang a song I had taught them.

When we were well-established as a performing group, I was contacted by the Public Television Channel at Texas State University. They wanted us to do a one-hour program with dance and explanation of the movements in the dance, along with some discussion about festivals and traditions of Japan. For the opening scene of the program, I planned a typical festival with music, drums, a portable shrine, a dragon, and a lot of action and dancing. We got creative with the portable shrine. I made a paper-mache Buddha using inflated balloons as the base and newspapers soaked in flour and water for the covering. One of the men students made the shrine and attached poles to be used for carrying it. We decorated it with folded paper streamers. Buddha was placed inside and looked majestic, surveying those who danced in front of him.

On the night of the show, we formed a caravan of cars and drove from San Antonio to Austin to the TV studio. CB radios were the latest craze at that time, and we kept in touch with each other on the way, although none of the cars strayed out of sight from each other. The CB conversations were fun and we had some good laughs. Other cars that were equipped with CBs joined in on the fun. It was a good way for the students to relax and forget their anxiety about performing in this production.

The studio had done a superb job of decorating the set, including a small red arched bridge over a serene pond and trees and cherry blossoms everywhere. Someone had done their homework and had transformed this large room into a miniature Japanese park at cherry blossom time.

Byron came with us to help with the driving and to take pictures. He was helpful to the dancers in many ways. Buz and Ken were drafted to walk around the balconies of the room and scatter paper cherry blossoms at appropriate times. They did a professional job. The blossoms floated down artistically.

The program opened with a scene of the still pond reflecting the bridge. A pebble was dropped into the middle of the pond and the ripples radiated to the banks as the Cherry Blossom song played softly. After an introduction in which I described a festival, the lively festival music started and the dancers came out with great enthusiasm, dancing and marching to the music, the shrine bearers carried the Buddha shrine, the dragon dashed and darted ahead of everyone.

There were intervals of solo and group dances preceded by my explanation of the various poses and fan movements and stories of the dances. The interviewer asked questions about customs and rituals. The hour passed quickly with no retakes, and we left for home well pleased with the outcome.

That show was televised many times over the next year. Unfortunately, the year was 1964 and VCRs had not yet been invented so we were unable to record it.

THE
PEOPLE
DANCE

One of the most delightful series of the season presents folk dances of America, and foreign lands—performed by dance groups of the central Texas area. THE PEOPLE DANCE is a KLRN production, directed by Bill Arhos. Sets and lighting by Lyle Hendricks and Bob Selby. Above, Masaka Collins, left, and Mrs. Byron Worther, instructor for the San Antonio Japanese Dancers, appear on the series. Below, the same organization performs the Ume Kawa Chub.

16

Page from TV Guide

Masako Collins and Alice

Fisherman's Dance

Cherry Blossom Dance

Silk Streamer Dance

Rice Picker's Dance

Carrying the Shrine

TV Show with my Youngest Students

43

The World Stood Still

WITHIN A FEW months after we settled into our house, the Cuban missile crisis unleashed the fear of another war, and we watched the developments on the newscasts. Byron, a senior air intelligence officer, was part of the intelligence force that was investigating the potential military threat to peace. He never could discuss his work with me, and I knew I couldn't ask him for any information. Thankfully, the situation ended peacefully.

A year later, we watched in disbelief as President Kennedy was shot while in an open car, waving to people who lined the streets in Dallas. Families huddled by their televisions for hours, mesmerized, waiting to hear if the president's wounds were fatal. The sad news was announced and a tearful nation was stricken with grief.

Schools and businesses closed. People stayed at home with their families. Still unable to accept the tragedy, we watched Jacky Kennedy, in her bloodstained pink suit, as she stood beside Lyndon Johnson while he was sworn into office as our next president.

Hour by hour, day by day, we watched the developments: the capture of Lee Harvey Oswald; Jack Ruby pushing his way through security guards to shoot and kill Oswald; Jacky in her mourning clothes, standing with her two small children beside her; the solemn funeral procession.

The nation watched, hypnotized, as it all unfolded live on television. Perhaps we watched so intensely because we weren't convinced that this was really happening.

Regardless of political preferences, all Americans mourned the loss of their president.

Byron was on the investigating team that searched Oswald's background and the possible link between Oswald and Ruby. This investigation took Byron away from home for weeks at a time.

Anyone who was born before 1953 can recall where they were the day President Kennedy was shot.

44

These Are Clean!

BYRON AND I were unprepared for this. Sometime between our last year in Japan and our first year in San Antonio, a metamorphosis had taken place. Our two oldest children had become teenagers. Our round-faced little Patty had transformed into a ravishing beauty.

Buz was getting taller.

One day while Patty was getting ready to go out with some friends, she noticed her period had started and she didn't have any supplies. She called out to Ken, gave him some money, and told him to run to the little store down the road and get her some sanitary napkins. Twenty minutes later, he returned with a package of paper dinner napkins. Ken was just twelve years old at the time. "Ken! I said *sanitary* napkins!" Patty shouted.

Ken, innocent and defensive, responded, "Well, *these* are clean!"

Patty, who now preferred to be called Pat, couldn't wait to get her driver's license. She hounded her father for lessons and he started her driver's education with his Volkswagen. He felt it was important that she learn how to shift gears.

She was having problems with jerky starts while she learned the clutch-gas relationship.

One Saturday afternoon as Byron turned on the TV to a football game, poured himself a glass of beer, and had just settled down to a relaxing afternoon, Patty begged him for a driving lesson. He gave in, but he brought his glass of beer with him. Patty started the ignition and proceeded with the gas pedal and clutch pedal ratio. The car jerked violently and Byron's beer splattered.

"Stop," he said, flicking off the drops of beer from his shirt and pants. "Get in the passenger seat. I'll show you how it's done."

"But, Dad, it's not me. There's something wrong with the car!" Patty (or Pat) defended herself.

"There's nothing wrong with the car. Now you watch this." He set the glass with the remaining beer on the dashboard. "I'm going to start this car and not one drop of beer is going to spill from that glass!" He turned on the ignition and started driving. The car jerked and the whole glass was airborne, dispensing its contents all over the car.

"Something's wrong with that car!" he muttered as he slammed the car door shut. That ended the lesson for that day.

She did get her license on her sixteenth birthday and she was an excellent driver. Byron received orders to go to Saigon, Vietnam, from March until September of 1965. Patty implored her father to let her have the Volkswagen for the summer while he was gone so she could get a job and earn money for a car of her own. She graduated from high school in June 1965 and would start as a freshman at Trinity University in September.

At first, Byron said no, but relented with the warning that she had better take good care of that car.

And so, Patty worked as a secretary during the summer and carefully put all her earnings in a savings bank. She drove the Volkswagen back and forth to work and, occasionally, to her boyfriend's house in the evenings.

One morning in late August, Patty went outside to start the car and came back in to announce the car wouldn't start. I went outside and raised the hood. I don't know why. I knew nothing about cars and had never driven the Volkswagen. I had my own Ford Falcon. "Well, no wonder it won't start! Someone stole your engine!" I announced.

Patty patiently said, "Mom, the engine is in the back." Checking the engine solved nothing for me, so I called a serviceman to come out and look at it. "Your engine has melted together," he said. Patty and I looked bewildered. "Haven't you been putting any oil in it?" he asked. Patty said, "Oh, so *that's* what that little green light was for."

"Can you fix it?" I asked.

"No, you need a whole new engine."

"How much is a new engine?"

The amount came to the exact amount of money Patty had earned during the summer to buy a used car. We looked at each other.

"Your father is coming home next week, you know."

"Yes, I know."

Patty paid for the new engine. It was installed the day before Byron arrived home.

Years later, Byron commented on how well his Volkswagen performed. "It drives just like it has a new engine!" he would say.

"It *has*," Patty would mutter.

Patty, Age 17

45

Good-bye, Dear Friend

ONE DAY, A few weeks after we moved into our new house, I was hanging laundry on the line in our backyard when a voice behind me broke the morning's silence.

"Hi, I'm Cynthia, your next door neighbor. We just moved in."

That accent! The inflection! Home! Home and all the people who talked like that. Home, the corner of the world I have seen only a few times since I left fifteen years ago.

Visions of quiet streets with canopies of green trees. Front porches where neighbors gathered on summer evenings. A bond was forming.

I turned and looked into smiling, sparkling eyes. "You're from Chicago," I said with certainty. "A suburb, yes," was the answer. The bond was completed. From that moment, we became close friends, sharing ideas, interests, and beliefs. We explored the city of San Antonio and went on shopping excursions together. We both found humor in ordinary situations, and our times together were filled with laughter.

Cynthia amazed me with her enthusiasm. When I phoned to invite her for morning coffee, she answered the phone with a cheerful hello. When I said, "Hi, Cynthia," she exploded with an exuberant, "Oh, hi, Alice!" I could feel her smile. She made me feel she was overjoyed that I had called.

Cynthia invited our family for Thanksgiving dinner that first year. The following year, we invited their family to our house for Thanksgiving dinner. We were all far away from our real families, so we became family to each other. Many evenings when we entertained friends, Cynthia and her husband, Al, joined us. Their cheerfulness always enlivened the gatherings.

Cynthia's daughter, Becky, was Buz's age. It was obvious she had a crush on him. One day as I was relaxing on my front porch, Becky came over to talk with me about Buz. "He doesn't seem to like me," she confided. "Is it because we're Jewish?" Her eyes pleaded for an honest answer. I looked at this innocent young girl and remembered the morning Cynthia knocked on my door and asked me to come look at the front of their house. I remembered staring in disbelief at the ugly hate words that were sprayed on their beautiful new house. Who would do such a thing?

That was over a year ago. This child still carried that hurt in her heart. Who knows what other past hurts were embedded in her memory? I reached out to her and assured her that religion was not a deterrent. "Buz is not intentionally ignoring you, Becky. He isn't thinking about girls yet. Right now, he's just interested in hanging out with his friends and going to car races. After all, you're both only fifteen." I wasn't so sure Buz wasn't thinking about girls, but I knew he was shy around them and certainly not ready to date.

Shortly after our two families celebrated our second Thanksgiving together, Cynthia was diagnosed with breast cancer. Surgery and treatments for cancer have improved greatly by 2011, but after Cynthia had surgery in 1964, it was discovered that the cancer had spread and there was nothing more that could be done.

They decided to spend her last weeks in Chicago, close to her sister and other family members. The night before they left, I helped her pack. She sat on her bed while I started to wrap her wedding picture. We looked at the beautiful happy young bride and the handsome groom. Cynthia said, "I thought he'd *never* get around to proposing marriage."

We were both quiet for a moment and she said, softly, "We made love before we were married." Was this a confession or just a confidence? I hugged her and said, "That doesn't count because you married him." We both chuckled. I finished wrapping the picture and placed it in her suitcase.

In the morning, we gathered on the driveway, embraced, kissed, and smiled. Byron handed Cynthia an envelope and told her not to open it until she was on the plane. We waved good-bye as the car backed out onto Fantasia Drive. When they were out of sight, the tears streamed down my face.

I asked Byron what was in the envelope he had given Cynthia. He said it was a Saint Christopher medal. He had enclosed a note that read:

> I know you are not Catholic. I am not Catholic either, but a friend gave me this medal the day I left for the war. I carried it all during the war. It was with me while we were being bombed at Pearl Harbor. Now I give it to you to keep you safe as you begin your journey.

Cynthia called us when she arrived in Chicago. She thanked Byron and said she would keep it near her. I called her several times while she was in the hospital. Each time she answered with "Oh, hi, Alice!" Her joy transcended the distance between us.

A few weeks later, Cynthia's light and laughter left this world. The next day, on the rose bush we had planted together between our houses bloomed a single beautiful peace rose. The pale golden petals slightly tinged with red were a tribute to her sunny disposition and her vibrancy.

46

It's June

F ATE ALWAYS CHOSE the month of June for us to move to a new location. It was a perfect month as the children were out of school, and we had the whole summer to make new friends and explore our new surroundings.

We have lived in San Antonio exactly four years. Patty has just finished her freshman year at college. Buz had worked after school and on weekends and finally saved enough to buy a used car. He will start his freshman year at Southwest Texas State University.

Ken has many friends and still catches frogs, but now he is fifteen and is spending time with a cute girl at the swimming pool. Barbara has just finished fourth grade and has diverse interests ranging from climbing trees with the boy next door to playing with dolls.

I had worked for three years at Trinity University as secretary to the chairman of the Biology Department. Our dance group continued to grow, and we were invited to dance at various functions. Byron completed twenty-five years of military service and retired a lieutenant colonel at the age of fifty.

Now it is June 1966. The movers just drove away. We have said good-bye to dear neighbors and are on our way to State College, Pennsylvania. But that's another story.

AFTERWORD

Women's Changing Roles

S EVENTY-FIVE YEARS AGO, before the inventions and situations that changed our lives, a married woman's role in society was very different from the lifestyle of today's woman.

I am describing my observations of the average woman's life in a small suburb of Chicago in 1935.

The husband's job at that time was to provide enough money to support his family. He was not expected to cook, clean or take care of the children. The wife was expected to stay at home and provide a clean house, clean clothes, and nourishing meals. She was the sole caretaker of the children. If a wife worked outside the house, it was a blow to her husband's pride and cast suspicions on his capability as a breadwinner.

During World War II, as the men left their jobs to enter the service, women took over many of those jobs and experienced a feeling of competency and independence. After the war, the men went back to their jobs or found new ones. Their wives went back to the home and housekeeping duties.

Separated for years by the war, the younger men and women didn't want to wait to marry until the man was established in a job, so they married and the wives worked while the men finished their college educations, subsidized by the G.I. Bill. The children of these marriages were called "The Baby Boomers".

In the 1950s and 1960s the rising cost of living made it necessary for wives to supplement their husband's income. New time-saving products and inventions helped to ease the transition for the housekeeper into the business world.

Gradually, through the following decades, women have found equality with men in almost every occupation and profession. Men have become more involved in the skills of housekeeping and the care of their children.

Both men and women have come a long way.

CPSIA information can be obtained at www.ICGtesting.com
Printed in the USA
LVOW110850140212

268589LV00003B/10/P